"I'm pregnant."

The air in Riley's lungs was sucked out of him. "I didn't see this one coming," he finally managed to say. "Hell, in the past two years, I haven't even been able to commit to a phone plan," he mumbled, a bit louder than he should have.

Tessa lifted her head, met his gaze and laughed. A single burst of pure uncut irony. "Riley, this isn't your problem."

Despite the jolt of the news, Riley didn't have any trouble carrying it to the next step. Tessa had already admitted it had been months since she'd had sex, so that meant the child had been conceived during the doctor's medical procedure.

"In case you have any doubts about how this will play out, the baby's mine," Riley said. Powerful words, life-changing words. Words he thought he'd never hear himself say.

"*Our* baby," he corrected.

MOMMY UNDER COVER

DELORES FOSSEN

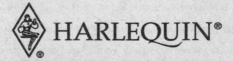

HARLEQUIN®

TORONTO • NEW YORK • LONDON
AMSTERDAM • PARIS • SYDNEY • HAMBURG
STOCKHOLM • ATHENS • TOKYO • MILAN • MADRID
PRAGUE • WARSAW • BUDAPEST • AUCKLAND

To Viki and Jan—thanks for being there

ISBN 0-373-22829-5

MOMMY UNDER COVER

Copyright © 2005 Delores Fossen

This edition published by arrangement with Harlequin Books S.A.

® and TM are trademarks of the publisher. Trademarks indicated with
® are registered in the United States Patent and Trademark Office, the
Canadian Trade Marks Office and in other countries.

www.eHarlequin.com

Printed in U.S.A.

ABOUT THE AUTHOR

Imagine a family tree that includes Texas cowboys, Choctaw and Cherokee Indians, a Louisiana pirate and a Scottish rebel who battled side by side with William Wallace. With ancestors like that, it's easy to understand why Texas author and former air force captain Delores Fossen feels as if she was genetically predisposed to writing romances. Along the way to fulfilling her DNA destiny, Delores married an air force top gun who just happens to be of Viking descent. With all those romantic bases covered, she doesn't have to look too far for inspiration.

CAST OF CHARACTERS

Agent Riley McDade—A Justice Department bad boy on assignment to bring down a murdering fertility specialist known as the Baby Maker, who was responsible for Riley's fiancée's death.

Agent Tessa Abbot—She's always played by the rules. She's a dedicated agent who's trying to climb to the top.

John Abbot—Tessa's father who's also a mission director in the Justice Department. Is he so desperate to collar a killer and clear his name that he's willing to risk Riley's and his daughter's lives?

Dr. Barton Fletcher—aka the Baby Maker. He's already murdered one federal agent who threatened to shut down his illegal medical procedures.

Prologue

Assisted Fertility Clinic
Dallas, Texas

"The Baby Maker," Dr. Barton Fletcher read from the personal memo clipped to the file.

So that's what people were calling him these days. He chuckled. It made him sound a little like God.

Which in a way, he was.

On occasion he'd created life. And on other occasions, he'd taken life. It all evened out in the end.

He glanced through the Tates' quarter-inch-thick file that his staff had put together for him. Aston Tate, a reclusive California software guru with an ego purportedly as large as his net worth, and his heiress wife, Isabel. Eccentric tendencies. Situational values and ethics.

In other words, his kind of people.

He'd been lucky finding *his kind of people.* Or

rather, they'd been lucky in finding him—all through word of mouth, of course. He couldn't advertise certain…aspects of his business. Not that lack of traditional advertisement had hurt. In the three short months the clinic had been open, he'd already assisted eleven couples with his procedure. The Tates would make it an even dozen.

Like the other eleven couples, the Tates were looking for a perfect baby. A baby genetically engineered to their specifications. Blond hair. Blue eyes. Male. Athletic build. Above average intelligence. *Well above* average. No imperfections of any kind.

In other words, the usual.

The hair and eye color varied from couple to couple, but the rest was a given.

There was something comforting about predictability.

Well, maybe.

Barton Fletcher took another look at the Tates' file.

The paperwork and requests were indeed predictable and in order, including the attached memo from Isabel Tate that lauded him as the Baby Maker for a couple who desperately wanted the child of their dreams. However, the fact that everything was in order did nothing to rid him of the knot tightening in his gut.

Was something wrong?

The obvious quickly came to mind. Maybe this

was some sort of sting operation. The latest attempt by authorities to apprehend him.

That wasn't going to happen.

Because he was always careful.

Always.

If these clients were indeed working for law enforcement, then he'd just have to deal with the situation as he had before.

Give life…take life. It all evened out in the end.

Chapter One

Agent Tessa Abbot walked into the briefing room of the Justice Department's Special Investigations Unit, took one look at him and came to a complete standstill.

Her steel-blue gaze riffled over his uncombed hair, down to his three-day-old beard. Possibly four.

Riley had lost count.

And then her gaze kept on riffling. Down to his scruffy black T-shirt, jungle fatigues and combat boots caked with mud. Thankfully the color of the T-shirt camouflaged a multitude of other stains that he didn't want to identify, but blood was a distinct possibility.

"Why are *you* here?" Tessa asked.

Riley lifted his hand in a wait-a-second gesture, gulped down the rest of his lukewarm coffee and prayed the caffeine would kick in soon. The all-night cargo flight from Liberia had left him with a wicked case of jet lag and the mother of all headaches.

"This is where I'm supposed to be. I'm your husband."

And with that, he waited for the excrement to hit the proverbial fan.

He didn't have to wait long.

"You're what?" Tessa adjusted her stance, shifting her weight from one fashionable snakeskin leather shoe to the other. Not her usual choice of footwear, which Riley knew for a fact tended toward something flat and more functional.

In her case, functional often included kick-butt, steel-toed boots.

This morning she was obviously dressed for the mission. And those three-inch-plus, mission-directed heels put her close to six feet tall.

Practically eye-to-eye with him.

That eye level allowed him to see her baby blues narrow significantly.

"I'm your husband," Riley repeated, even though he was dead certain she'd heard him the first time. "Well, your husband for this mission, anyway. After I get cleaned up, we'll be the undercover team going into the Assisted Fertility Clinic in Dallas."

Somehow, Riley managed to say that without any emotion. Inside—well, that was a whole different story. There was emotion, all right. Lots of it. And he intended to channel all those still-raw feelings into apprehending Dr. Barton Fletcher, aka the Baby Maker.

"You're mistaken." And Tessa didn't say it with affection, either. No surprise there. This would not be an affection-generating conversation. "I'm teamed with Agent Trapanna for this."

So the mission commander hadn't informed her yet. Riley was afraid of that. That meant he'd have to be the messenger. Not his first choice of duties for 0600 hours. Or any other hour for that matter.

"There's been a change in plans," Riley explained. "Trapanna came down with some kind of throat infection last night. He's on antibiotics and bed rest. I heard what happened and volunteered to fill in for him."

That *heard-what-happened* part was really glossing over things.

For days Riley had been calling for permission updates on the Baby Maker case. It'd been no accident that he'd learned of Trapanna's medical condition and within five minutes had arranged a flight out of Liberia. Of course, he'd had to finish a really nasty confrontation with two armed guerrillas before he could get to the airport—hence the possibility of blood on his shirt. *Their* blood. But he'd made it back to D.C. in time for the mission brief.

Tessa stared at him. And stared. Apparently processing his impromptu situation report. Judging from the way the muscles stirred and jumped in her blush-touched cheeks, she didn't process it well.

"You volunteered?" she questioned.

Riley settled for a nod.

"Oh, mercy." She groaned, tossed her mission folder onto the conference table and aimed her index finger at him. "Let's get something straight. I don't want you anywhere near this ops, got that?"

As Riley guessed she would do, Tessa reached for the sleek black phone on the wall. Probably so she could call the mission director and complain about the turn of events. Riley didn't want that to happen.

Not yet anyway.

Some fast talking and lots of luck had gotten him this ops and he wasn't about to let Tessa Abbot take it away from him.

There was too much at stake.

Riley deposited his empty foam cup onto the table and, in the same motion, caught her arm—a little maneuver that earned him a glare. Man, she was good at it, too. Those steely eyes practically tapered to slits as she shook off his grip.

"If you've got a problem with our working together, then say it to me," Riley insisted. "Not to our boss."

Without even a second's hesitation, she gave him an *Okay, I will* nod. "Oh, I have a problem, all right.

A huge one. There's no way you can be objective about Dr. Barton Fletcher, and you and I both know why."

Riley didn't hesitate, either. "I'll take a wild guess here and assume you're referring to the fact that Fletcher killed my former partner?"

It wasn't a wild guess.

That was exactly what this was about.

"Fletcher *allegedly* killed your former partner," Tessa amended, using the politically correct term. "Your fiancée."

"Your friend," Riley added.

Just in case Tessa had forgotten.

Even though he knew she hadn't.

He was reasonably sure that no one in SIU had forgotten.

Riley scrubbed his hand over his face. "And there's nothing 'allegedly' about it. Fletcher murdered Colette. The only thing missing is the proof. Proof I intend to find so I can put the SOB on death row where he belongs."

Now, there was emotion. Riley couldn't possibly contain it this time. It was like a fist clamped around his heart. Squeezing the life right out of him.

But then, Colette had been the woman he'd loved.

The woman he had planned to spend the rest of his life loving. The woman he'd asked to marry him just hours before that last mission nearly two years ago. And he had allowed his love for Colette and their personal relationship to distract him at the worst possible time. That distraction had given Dr. Barton Fletcher the opportunity to kill her.

"Exactly my point," Tessa countered. "Fletcher murdered someone close to you. That only proves your inability to be objective about this case."

"You were close to her, too, Tessa," Riley quickly pointed out.

She shook her head. "I wasn't engaged to her. Big difference. I'm talking huge."

Riley calmly leaned closer. "And do you think my feelings for Colette make me less or more eager to bring Fletcher down?"

Tessa leaned closer, as well, until they were only inches apart. "I think it makes you a huge liability and therefore a dangerous one."

Okay. So they'd moved on to the pull-no-punches mode. That was his preferred mode of operation anyway. "I could say the same about you. You were just as shaken by Colette's murder as I was."

"Yes." Tessa repeated it and took a deep breath. "But you have a choice about being here." She jabbed that perfectly manicured index finger against his chest and leaned in. "I. Don't."

It was true. On the flight from Liberia, he'd read all about it in the preliminary mission report. Riley had been waiting for nearly two years for Dr. Barton Fletcher to reopen his business.

Two long years.

And the moment it happened, Riley had started the networking that would hopefully give him a shot at getting a coveted appointment with the murdering doctor. However, Tessa beat him to him. Not intentionally. While she'd been working on another case, she'd stumbled onto a contact that had offered to help get her that appointment.

Blind luck, some would say.

But even if it was luck, fate, karma—whatever, Riley intended to use it and any other opportunity that came his way to catch Fletcher.

"What if Fletcher recognizes you, huh?" Tessa asked, obviously trying a different angle.

"He won't. I've never even met the man. I was stuck in a surveillance van during Colette's last mission." Riley had to pause a moment before he could finish. "By the time I got to her, Fletcher and his hired assassins were long gone."

And Colette was dead.

That brought back the flood of memories. The nightmare. He couldn't make that nightmare go away, ever, but he could try to get some justice for Colette.

"Any other objections?" Riley challenged.

Silence.

Not coupled with a glare, either, which didn't make it any easier to take. Because he was almost positive he saw some disgust in her eyes. And worse, he saw sympathy, as well.

"Go ahead," Riley insisted in a rough whisper. "Say it—you blame me for Colette's death."

Tessa dodged his gaze and stepped to the side, the sleeve of her precisely fitted indigo-blue silk jacket sliding against his mud-splattered arm. What she didn't do was *say it*. No reminder of the fact that during that deadly assignment, he'd violated regulations by not excusing himself from a mission where he'd been intimately involved with his partner.

It had been a mistake.

One he'd regret for the rest of his life.

And one he wouldn't repeat.

"This isn't just about Colette," Tessa said—finally. "I don't like working with agents who make a habit of bending the rules. And let's face it, Riley. You don't just bend the rules, you break them. Often."

Not exactly the heavy-fisted admonishment she could have hurled at him. But, like her semisympathetic eyes, it pushed a few buttons. Mainly because it questioned his competence. His rogue instincts had saved his butt on several occasions—and he was good at his job.

Damn good.

"You think Dr. Barton Fletcher will play by the rules, Tessa?" Riley shook his head. "I doubt it. In fact,

I think he'd prefer being investigated by a yes-sir operative who can't or won't think outside the box."

She mumbled some profanity under her breath. Since he was still close enough to smell her pricey mission-required perfume, Riley had no trouble hearing that profanity—which was mainly directed at him.

So he'd made his point.

If the point he was trying to make was that they could both be smart-asses.

That wasn't a good thing since they'd have to work together. Plus, to bring Fletcher down, he needed her help and she needed his. A little fact that obviously wouldn't make either of them happy.

Forcing himself to do some damage control, Riley caught her silk-covered arm again and eased her around to face him.

"Look, we have different approaches to what we do." He kept his voice level. Or rather, tried to. "That's not necessarily a bad thing. And even if it were, it's no longer an issue. We're partners. *Period.*"

Judging from Tessa's Arctic stare, she would have almost certainly challenged that—again—if the door to the meeting room hadn't swung open. No knock. But Riley hadn't expected the lanky, ginger-haired guest to announce his presence with a customary knock.

The man was John Abbot, the mission commander for this particular ops, and therefore their boss.

He was also Tessa's father.

Abbot spared them both a glance, barely, before he flipped open a laptop and dropped down into the high-backed, burgundy-leather chair at the head of the conference table. "Let's make this quick. I have two other missions launching today—"

"Sir, I'd like to request a different partner," Tessa interrupted.

"Request denied." Abbot didn't even look at her, choosing instead to keep his attention fastened to the laptop screen. "Riley McDade's the only agent with deep-cover experience who was available on such short notice."

"Yes. But in my opinion, Riley's much too close to the case."

This time John Abbot's eyes slid in their direction. Eyes that were an exact copy of the woman stewing next to him. Oh, yeah. Abbot could do that glare thing as well as Tessa.

She'd obviously learned from the master.

"Everyone in SIU is close to the case," Abbot snapped. "It was my call to put Riley on the team." He paused for a heartbeat. "A call he'd better not make me regret."

And with that gruffly barked reprimand, Abbot motioned for them to sit. It wasn't a request, either. Riley took the chair on the left; Tessa sat on the other side of the table. Directly across. Probably so she could still glare at him.

Abbot volleyed glances at both of them. Paused. Mumbled something. "Is it necessary for me to remind you two that you're posing as a happily married couple who desperately want a baby?"

Riley looked at her.

Tessa looked at him.

"No reminder necessary," Riley assured their boss.

Even though they might have to remind each other.

"Good." Abbot turned his attention back to the computer screen where he was no doubt scanning the latest intel report. "Judging from what we've been able to hear with our monitoring equipment, you can expect to establish your first face-to-face contact with Dr. Fletcher this afternoon at fifteen hundred hours. He'll probably go over the records we've created for you, but beyond that, we're not sure what'll be asked of you. Some lab tests, maybe. Perhaps more."

It was that "more" part that had given Riley a few uncomfortable thoughts. Mainly because he didn't know what "more" would entail. With Fletcher, it could be just about anything. Still, that wouldn't stop him.

"I take it there are no pictures in the records you created for us?" Tessa asked. But there was a little too much hope in her tone for it not to set Riley's teeth on edge. She obviously hadn't given up on ditching him.

She was wasting her time.

"No pictures," Abbot confirmed. "The Tates are

supposed to be camera-shy recluses because they fear kidnapping attempts. But there are some fake bios in the records and the lab results from the tests Fletcher's staff ran on you earlier this week. Plus, there are probably some extensive background checks that Fletcher had done."

Tessa's eyebrow lifted a fraction, the lift apparently aimed at Riley.

"I've studied the mission folder," Riley volunteered. "I know what I'm supposed to do."

"I'm sure you do," Abbot interjected, pausing barely a second. "Neither of you will be able to carry a weapon or a communication device inside the clinic. With Fletcher's extensive security measures, it'd be too risky. But we'll have a team in the area monitoring you, and if something goes wrong, they'll respond as needed."

In other words, evasive measures. And there was absolutely no guarantee that those evasive measures would be effective, enough, or in time. If their cover didn't hold, it could turn ugly.

Just as it had the day Colette was murdered.

That reminder was like a sucker punch. Riley quickly shoved it aside to concentrate on the briefing.

"Any indication that Fletcher is suspicious of us?" Tessa asked.

Abbot shook his head. "Just the opposite. From what we can tell, his people have dug no further than the records we provided."

That was something at least. It meant they weren't walking into a trap.

"While you're at the clinic, Fletcher will arrange a time for the second appointment that should happen within the next seventy-two hours," Abbot went on. "Well, hopefully he'll do that. For that appointment, Fletcher will take you to an unspecified facility where we believe he's been performing the medical procedures."

Not a simple in vitro or insemination for couples having trouble conceiving. Oh, no.

During these medical procedures, Dr. Barton Fletcher would supposedly manipulate the DNA to get the made-to-specs designer babies that rich, self-absorbed couples wanted.

And it was that made-to-specs part that made what he did highly illegal.

If Riley couldn't pin a murder rap on the doctor, then he'd see how long he could put Fletcher behind bars for performing illegal medical procedures.

"One more thing," Abbot added. "Riley will be the team leader for this assignment."

Okay. Riley hadn't thought there'd be any more surprises today, but obviously he'd been wrong.

Tessa pulled in a hard breath. "But—"

"Riley's had more experience in deep-cover ops." There was an unspoken "I won't budge on this" at the end of Abbot's comment. "And deep cover is exactly what I want the two of you to maintain once you leave headquarters. Remember, after you arrive for your appointment this afternoon, Fletcher will almost certainly keep you under tight surveillance."

In other words, continue to play the part of the loving couple. No easy task since they were practically at each other's throats.

"Questions?" Abbot asked, standing. "Doubts? Concerns? Complaints?"

As if they would actually voice any of that to him. They'd both already fulfilled their complaint quota for the day. Maybe for their entire careers as federal agents.

Tessa and Riley shook their heads.

Abbot closed the laptop, got up and headed for the door. But then he stopped and turned back around. He aimed his attention at Tessa.

"The chief is still considering your promotion. I'll make my recommendation to him after this mission."

With that, Abbot made his exit and the door swished closed behind him.

"A promotion?" Riley mumbled. "And it probably hinges on this ops. No pressure there, huh?"

Tessa was already reaching for the mission folder, but her hand stopped in midreach. "And do you think that makes this ops more, or less, important to me?" she countered, throwing his own words right back at him.

Riley couldn't help it. He had to smile. "Dare I use

the P-word? As in *personal?* Seems to me that you have a problem with agents going into an ops when there's something personal at stake."

"This is a mission," Tessa informed him, sounding very much as if she were trying to convince herself. "And I don't bring personal issues into a mission."

He was betting she would this time.

Tessa and he had both been friends with Colette. That made it personal. Added to that, they had to spend the next few days in close, intimate quarters pretending to be a loving, married couple.

And they had to do it with a killer watching their every move.

Oh, yeah.

That was just about as personal—and as dangerous—as things could get.

Chapter Two

Thanks to some road construction, the limo was crawling through the congested Dallas traffic. The stop-and-go snail's pace didn't help the tension that had settled in the back of Tessa's neck. Of course, she couldn't blame that tension solely on the traffic, the circuitous clandestine flights they'd taken from D.C. or even the mission itself.

No.

That tension had a lot to do with the man in the black cashmere sweater who was seated shoulder-to-shoulder with her.

Her *partner.*

Her *husband.*

And the absolute last agent she wanted to be paired with for this mission.

Tessa had planned for a lot of contingencies, but Riley McDade sure wasn't one of them.

She wanted a quick in and out. No complications. Nothing to extend the length of this ops.

And especially nothing to interfere with its success.

With his renegade tendencies, personal chip on his shoulder and badass attitude, Riley McDade put all those things in question.

"The fictional Aston Tate was born in L.A.," she heard Riley say. Not to her. He was obviously going over the undercover identity info stored on his Palm-Pilot. "He's twenty-nine—just two years younger than me, so I shouldn't have a problem with that. He collects Civil War memorabilia—I'll have to fake that part. He's a huge L.A. Lakers fan—won't have to fake that. And he's a jackass."

Tessa glanced at the PalmPilot he had cradled in his hand. "It says that in the file?"

He shook his head. "No, that's my opinion. Anybody who'd go to these lengths to have the perfect heir is a jackass. He should be satisfied with what Mother Nature intended him to have. Or not have."

That tension in her neck went up a notch.

Tessa decided it was a good time to sit quietly and stare out the limo window. Maybe that way she wouldn't have to respond to Riley's comment, but her silence didn't do a thing to ease the deep ache in her heart.

"I'm pulling into the parking lot of the clinic now,"

Chris Ingram, the limo driver and fellow SIU agent, informed them through the intercom.

It was almost show time. Tessa took a deep breath. Steadying herself. And hating that steadying herself was even necessary. Why had fate chosen her for this assignment anyway? Talk about rubbing salt in a wound.

A baby mission.

One where she had to pretend to be a hopeful parent who desperately wanted to conceive the perfect child. Well, at least she wouldn't have to fake the desperately-wanted-to-conceive part. All she had to do was open a vein and let her true feelings flow. In that respect, she was the ideal agent for this ops.

Tessa clung to that.

And hoped it was enough to get her through.

Because in another respect, she was as ill-suited for this as Riley was.

Maybe even more.

Both of them had more than enough emotional baggage to sink this mission before it even got off the ground. And for her, it was emotional baggage that she should have gotten rid of years ago. Bottom line: a baby couldn't change what had happened in her own childhood. It couldn't change what her father and she had endured because her mother had walked out on them when she was a child. It couldn't change any of that. But the emotional baggage could definitely interfere with what she needed to do now on this mission.

If she let it interfere, that is.

She wouldn't.

Riley clicked off the PalmPilot, essentially erasing its memory. A necessary security precaution. "Want to practice your bio?" he asked.

"Not really." She already had it committed to memory. Isabel Tate. Twenty-nine. Tessa's own age. No hobbies. No real life—something that Tessa could definitely relate to. Isabel was essentially the reclusive trophy wife of an equally reclusive trophy husband. A marriage of new money and blue blood.

"There'll be lots of personal contact between us when we're in there," Riley commented. "And afterward while we're at the second appointment."

"I know. Loving couple and all that. I understand what we have to do, Riley."

He nodded. Paused. And otherwise continued to grill her with those storm-gray eyes. "You haven't been in a deep-cover situation like this before."

That improved her posture. He'd better not be questioning her abilities. Or reminding her that her father had appointed him as team leader.

"Are you trying to make conversation or a point?" she asked.

"Definitely a point. At a minimum, we'll probably have to kiss while Fletcher has us under surveillance."

Oh, that.

She'd thought about kisses all right, along with other intimate behavior that might be expected of a happily married couple.

Embraces.

Long, lingering looks.

Caresses.

It wouldn't be especially comfortable. Or easy. But then, there wasn't much about this assignment that would be easy. Still, she'd do it. There were a lot worse things than kissing Riley.

With that reminder, she glanced at his mouth. Sensual, she supposed. After another glance, Tessa took out the *supposed.* Yes, his mouth was sensual, and why the heck she'd noticed it, she didn't know.

"Well?" Riley prompted when they stepped out of the limo.

"Well, what?" Tessa asked, already worried that her daydreams about his mouth had caused her to miss something important.

He mumbled some profanity and wiped his hand through his stealth black hair that fell several inches down his neck. The swipe and the gusty October wind only mussed it more, but it still managed to look fashionably disheveled. A term that actually described his overall appearance.

"You understand what we might have to do in there, right?" he asked, obviously irritated.

"It's not an issue," she assured him, tossing that irritation right back at him. "If the situation dictates a kiss, then kiss away."

But both knew it might not be limited to just a kiss.

After all, they were about to enter a fertility clinic. Where virtually anything could be expected of them. *Anything.* And the man who'd be expecting it was the very person who'd created a dark cloud over the Special Investigations Unit. He'd killed one of their own and gotten away with it.

So far.

As long as Fletcher was free, the dark cloud would stay. Over Riley. Over her father. Over the entire department.

And she could do something about that.

She could finally rid her father of the one black mark on his otherwise spotless career record: his failure to close out Colette's murder.

Maybe then...

"Where are you right now?" she heard Riley whisper. There was yet more annoyance in his voice. He slipped his arm around her waist and eased her closer to him. Not exactly a loving gesture, either. He gave her a nudge.

Tessa glanced at him and was on the verge of asking him what he meant, but those raised questioning eyebrows said it all.

"I'm focused," she assured him.

He made a sound to indicate he didn't believe her.

She made a sound to indicate she didn't care what he thought.

It was going to be a long mission.

They entered the brownstone building and Tessa paused in the doorway. To get her bearings. To observe. To make sure she was indeed focused.

She counted three security cameras in the reception area. Not two, as stated in the intel report. That meant the surveillance team hadn't known about the recent modifications in the clinic.

Tessa silently cursed.

She'd already had enough surprises on this ops without adding yet another.

"Camera in the corner above the fake Picasso," Riley muttered.

"I saw it. And I don't think it's a fake."

Definitely not the decor or security measures for a typical fertility clinic. But then, Dr. Barton Fletcher was nowhere in the range of being typical.

There were no other patients. Just a brunette receptionist whose brass nameplate on her practically bare, glass-topped desk identified her as Beatrice Holden. The woman was almost certainly a hired gun. Tessa noticed the faint outline of a shoulder holster beneath her loose mocha-colored jacket.

"The Tates, I presume," Beatrice concluded, her more than mildly curious gaze raking over them. She hitched her shoulder in the direction of a hall. "Follow me."

They did. Down the wide corridor that Tessa knew from studying the floor plans would end at the sitting area outside Fletcher's office. They passed no other visible doors along the way, but there were some concealed ones behind the judge's paneling that didn't quite go with the rest of the decor. Likely spots for escape routes.

Or security guards.

The fact she didn't have a weapon suddenly made Tessa very uncomfortable. Riley must have felt the same way because the muscles tensed in his arm that he had curved around her waist. Because of Colette and his obsession with getting revenge, there was no telling what kind of emotional wringer he was going through at the moment.

As they neared the end of the hall, the doctor stepped out from the sitting area and flashed them a slick smile that sent a chill snaking down her spine.

Tessa hadn't been sure how she'd react to Barton Fletcher, but she was a firm believer in instincts. In this case her instincts confirmed what everyone already suspected: the man was a killer.

Too bad the justice system required more than her instincts as proof. And too bad that hard evidence was the very thing they lacked. Of course, that was what this mission was all about—gathering evidence to bring a killer to justice.

Like the reception area, the sitting room outside his office was plush. Decorated with original artwork and a Turkish rug that was probably worth six figures.

But that wasn't all.

On one wall there were framed black-and-white photos. Artistically done. Precisely placed. All of babies. Lots of babies. Some were newborns snuggled into blankets. Others were slightly older with round smiling faces.

Tessa cursed herself when she had to take another deep breath.

That deep breath sent Riley's gaze sliding in her direction. "Are you okay?" he whispered. *Lovingly* whispered. He pressed a husbandly kiss on her cheek.

It was time to open that vein a little.

Not that she could have possibly kept it closed anyway.

Tessa tipped her head toward the photos. "Aren't they beautiful?" She made sure her voice cracked a little. It wasn't difficult to do.

Riley nodded, his interest not on the photos but still on her. His stare, along with his slightly tightened grip, was a subtle question. What the heck was wrong with her? But it was also a subtle warning for her to keep her attention on the mission.

"The babies are a few of my many success stories," Dr. Fletcher volunteered.

Thankfully, the doctor's voice dragged Tessa back to where she needed to be. She forced aside the old wounds, the old issues, and reminded herself that she couldn't do anything about the past, but she could do something about the future.

The doctor led them into his office. Fletcher obviously had expensive taste and his workplace wasn't the only thing that reflected it. His clothes were flawless, along with being pricey. Somehow, the classic conservative Italian suit didn't clash with the eraser-size diamond stud in his right earlobe.

"Thank you for coming on such short notice," Fletcher offered.

"We wouldn't have missed this." Riley eased onto the sofa across from Fletcher's desk. Tessa followed and stayed close. "Our future son is our number-one priority."

"Your future son is important to me, as well." Fletcher sat at his desk and typed in something on his computer keyboard. "When I meet with potential clients for the first time, I start with the basics. Many couples come to me for enhanced conceptions, but because my time is limited, I'm selective about those I agree to help."

Tessa didn't have to fake a surprised reaction to that. Her response was completely natural. A week before at her preliminary screening, Fletcher's medical technician had told her that once a couple was granted an actual appointment with the doctor, that meant they'd been approved for the procedure. The only thing left to finalize the deal should have been the quarter-million-dollar fee.

Had Fletcher changed his policy about that?

"You *are* going to help us?" she asked.

Fletcher didn't respond right away. Nor did he look at them. He kept his gaze fastened to his computer screen. Unfortunately, Tessa couldn't see what had garnered his attention, but it sent her heart pounding. Mercy. They'd come too close for him to stop things now.

"I always request background checks on potential clients," Fletcher explained, ignoring her question. "You both obviously value your privacy. It took my assistants days to delve through the layers of cyber security."

Okay.

That didn't do much to return her heart rate back to normal. Especially since only hours earlier her father had assured them that Fletcher hadn't taken much interest in their backgrounds.

Just how far had Fletcher's "assistants" delved?

And what had they learned?

"Well?" Riley questioned. However, he didn't just question. He took her by the hand and stood as if preparing to leave. "If you're not going to help us, Doc, then we'll have to find someone else who will. Come on, darling."

Tessa stood, as well, wondering if they would have to fight their way out of here. If Fletcher was on to them, he wouldn't just let them leave.

She watched Fletcher's hand carefully. Bracing herself in case he reached for a gun in his desk drawer.

But he didn't reach for anything. Fletcher motioned for Riley to sit back down. "Of course, I'll help you, Mr. Tate. The background check was simply a square filler, and now that it's complete, we can move on to the next square."

Tessa hoped her sigh of relief wasn't too audible.

So, they were in.

Whatever *in* entailed.

The doctor turned back to his computer. "I've gone over your wife's lab results, and the best time for us to begin the procedure is three days from now. How does that fit into your schedule?"

Tessa looked at Riley. They both paused, pretending to think about it. And then both nodded.

"Good," Fletcher concluded. "On the evening of the twelfth, I'll send a car for you. You'll be at the address you listed on your original paperwork?"

"Yes," Riley and Tessa answered in unison.

It was an estate located in the heart of Dallas, just

a few miles away. Their Justice Department agency, the SIU, had rented it for them to use to maintain their cover as the wealthy Tates. According to the latest intel report, Fletcher's people had already gained access to the exterior of the property by posing as groundskeepers and had installed video-surveillance equipment in the back and side gardens. That meant any time Riley or she walked past a window, they'd need to play the part of the Tates.

"For the next appointment, you'll be taken to a clinic where I'll be waiting for you," Fletcher continued. "I insist the location be kept secret. You'll tell no one where you're going. Please don't let that alarm you. I ask this of all my patients."

"Why all the security precautions?" Tessa asked, because she thought it was something any normal person would want to know.

The doctor drummed his fingers against his desk and eased his perfectly shaped mouth into another of those oily smiles. "There are those who object to the services I provide."

A huge understatement, and not really a truthful one, but Tessa only gave him a sympathetic nod.

Fletcher returned the nod. "The clinic will be secure, and I'm certain all of us will be more comfortable in a secure location where we won't be interrupted."

Or arrested.

That was no doubt the real reason for keeping the clinic's location a closely guarded secret. Since those medical procedures were illegal, Fletcher wouldn't want to risk being caught while actually performing one.

"Before you leave today, we'll need to do some blood work." Fletcher then transferred his attention to Riley. "And for you, we'll need semen. Your wife can accompany you to the private area of the lab to do the collection, but we do need the specimen *inside the cup* and not elsewhere."

The doctor chuckled. Tessa and Riley added their own sounds of amusement, as well.

So, this was one of those "loving couple and all that" contingencies.

Riley brought her hand to his mouth and kissed lightly. When their gazes met, there was some mild humor in his eyes. "I'll go solo for the collection. Having you in there with me would be a little too, uh, tempting."

Relief washed through her. She was willing to do a lot to make sure this mission succeeded, but she truly hadn't wanted to witness *that.*

"Will we be staying overnight at your other facility?" she asked the doctor.

"Absolutely. It might be several days before I can do the final surgical procedure with the modified embryo."

A procedure that wouldn't happen.

There was no way she could let things progress to the point where she was having actual surgery. If Riley and she didn't have the evidence they needed by then, they'd have to come up with some excuse and get out of there. Surgery would basically immobilize her and make her highly vulnerable to just about anything Fletcher wanted to do to her.

Including murder.

"We'll be able to take a tour of the facility first?" Riley questioned.

"No tours." There wasn't a shred of hesitation in Fletcher's voice. "Again, for security reasons, I don't even give out the address."

Okay, that wasn't the ideal scenario for an undercover ops, but it was what she'd expected. Now, at least, they were within days of identifying the location and getting inside it.

Not a bad start.

Fletcher reached across the desk and handed Riley a single sheet of paper. "That's our agreement, which I'll ask you both to sign. It spells out the issues we've already discussed."

It also spelled out the fee. A hundred thousand dollars in advance, and it was to be paid with a cashier's check to an unnamed representative who would be transporting them to the first clinic.

In other words, Fletcher was at least one step removed from the money trail. Ditto for the final payment. That was to be electronically transferred to a foreign bank account within six hours of the final medical procedure. And it was to be paid whether it was successful or not.

Fletcher handed Riley a pen. "If you agree, please sign at the bottom."

Riley scrawled his fake signature and passed it to her. Tessa glanced over it. Not that she planned to object to anything and not that there was anything too specific for her to object to. The wording was vague—except for the payment part. Tessa signed it, as well, and placed it on Fletcher's desk.

"We're all set to go then," Fletcher confirmed, returning his attention to her. "Once you two arrive at the clinic, you'll immediately be prepped and tested for Phase One of Project Ideal Baby. After that, I'll take you to the actual medical facility where we'll be doing the remainder of the procedures."

Tessa didn't care much for those words, *prepped* and *tested,* especially when they were combined with the time frame of *immediately.*

Obviously, Riley picked up on it, as well. Their gazes met again. In the swirls of all of those shades of gray, she saw the same concerns that were no doubt mirrored in her own eyes. This was not a contingency they'd expected.

"What exactly is Phase One?" Riley asked the doctor.

Fletcher shrugged as if it were unimportant. "A simple artificial insemination."

Tessa was absolutely sure she blinked.

She hoped that was her only visible reaction.

"Insemination?" she repeated. Not easily, either. "I thought there'd be some sort of egg harvesting?"

Which obviously would take longer than *immediately*.

In fact, egg harvesting would take weeks or even months. That'd give them more than enough time to search the clinic before having to come up with an excuse as to why they couldn't have an in vitro, or any other procedure, done.

"Egg harvesting shouldn't be necessary," the doctor explained. "The insemination is a much simpler process. No anesthesia required, and it's no more invasive than a routine gynecological exam."

Fletcher stood and went to the door. Probably his cue for them to leave.

Tessa stood, as well, but she had no plans to leave just yet. Not until she had some answers. "But why would I even need to be inseminated?"

"To become pregnant, of course. Don't worry," Fletcher assured her. Coming from him, of course, it was no assurance at all. "Our goal is for you to conceive as quickly as possible. Then the real work starts. Well, for me, anyway, with the DNA manipulation. Within two weeks, maybe less, there's at least a fifty percent chance that you'll already be pregnant with the child of your dreams."

Wrong.

There was *no* chance.

But that hasty insemination could jeopardize this entire undercover case.

Mercy.

"I'm probably stating the obvious here, but if my wife becomes pregnant through insemination, how will we get our perfect baby?" Riley asked, his voice sounding considerably sturdier than Tessa suddenly felt.

"I'll remove the embryo, perform the DNA manipulation and then replace it in utero."

Even though she wasn't a doctor, Tessa was somewhat well versed in fertility procedure. And she was pretty certain that the DNA manipulation after conception wasn't medically possible.

In other words, this was a scam.

Jeez.

That was both good news and bad news. Good, because it meant the doctor wasn't really doing any DNA manipulation. Bad, because the scam still involved a medical procedure. It meant headquarters might not approve continuation of the mission once they learned she'd have to submit herself to artificial insemination to gain closer access to Fletcher's facilities.

However, if she stopped things now, it might take another team months to get an appointment with Fletcher.

If at all. And he could end up walking away.

Tessa took another look at the doctor. Her instincts screamed that this man needed to be stopped. Somehow. Even if it was just on fraud charges.

And she was the one who could do it. "Couldn't we just do this the old-fashioned way, Doctor? And call you once I'm pregnant?"

"Unfortunately, Mrs. Tate, this is a very time-sensitive procedure. Both on the embryo's part and mine. It works best if you are carefully monitored from the moment of insemination and, hopefully, conception. Otherwise, when you discover you're pregnant, I may not be available and/or the embryo may already be too old for the procedures."

Tessa didn't know how she could argue with that and still appear to be a woman desperate for one of Dr. Fletcher's babies. "All right," she said.

Riley's gaze snapped toward her. *"All right?"*

"You heard what Dr. Fletcher said," Tessa reiterated, adding a nervous laugh. She didn't have to fake the nervous part, either. "The insemination's necessary, and the end result won't be…well, an ordinary baby. So, of course, we'll do it."

All that was left was to convince headquarters— and Riley—that the success of this mission hinged on her agreeing to this simple procedure.

No easy task.

Especially since the procedure would be performed by a killer.

Chapter Three

Riley stood in the marbled foyer of the estate and waited while Tessa ran the detector wand over every inch of her clothes.

Not once, but twice.

When she finished, she passed the detector his way and Riley did the same.

No telltale soft beeps, which he hoped meant Fletcher hadn't managed to attach some type of monitoring device to either Tessa or him.

Other than a phony, laughter-punctuated conversation in the limo about the upcoming joys of parenthood, Tessa and he had yet to talk. *Really* talk. Unfortunately that would have to continue a while longer, even though he had some questions. Well, one question in particular. They also had to give a situation report to their mission commander.

Another potential problem.

The commander had no doubt monitored their

limo conversation to ascertain if they were indeed safe, but since neither Tessa nor he had mentioned the insemination, no one back at headquarters had a clue as to what they were up against.

Soon, they would.

And this mission could be terminated.

The possibility sickened him. He desperately wanted to bring Dr. Barton Fletcher to justice, and that wouldn't happen if the mission stalled. Of course, if it didn't stall, there was that whole other issue.

A whopper of an issue.

A potential baby. A real one.

Oh, man.

Talk about the ultimate complication. That was something they'd definitely have to get straight.

He damn sure hadn't signed on to this ops to become a parent.

"Wanna play in the shower?" Tessa asked, making it sound like a carnal invitation to her husband instead of a required security measure for her partner.

"I'd love to."

Translation? *Let's wash any potential transmitter chips off before we talk.*

Tessa took the modified suitcase from beneath the antique table in the foyer and started to shed her clothes. Riley turned his back to her and did the same.

Tossing in an occasional seductive laugh and more of those mumbled sweet nothings, they stripped down to their underwear and put their clothes in the suitcase. After they were in the shower, the rookie SIU agent, Chris Ingram, who was posing as the butler-houskeeper-chauffeur, would whisk the suitcase away so it could be analyzed.

"Are you sure you're up to this?" Tessa purred. She headed toward the stairs. "I mean, after your, uh, little donation at the clinic?"

"The donation in no way lessened my appetite for you, darling."

From over her shoulder she gave him a "good one" nod. Probably her idea of placating him.

It wouldn't work.

He was still riled about that "all right" response she'd given to Fletcher about the insemination. They should have pressed the issue, then and there. They should have found a way around it, then and there. But instead, Tessa had closed down the discussion with her little "all right."

And this from the woman who just that morning had raked him over the coals about bending rules.

What the heck had she been thinking anyway?

Riley intended to find that out as soon as they finished showering, but a confrontation with her was still minutes away. Minutes to think about how they were going to get out of this one.

He was still in the middle of his own personal but silent gripe session when he glanced at Tessa on the steps just ahead of him. Specifically he glanced at her underwear. Sturdy cotton. White, at that. No provocative lace or silk. No barely there swatches. No padded, push-up anything. Just a plain white bra and a pair of panties.

Hell.

And what was he doing noticing that?

Riley cursed.

Obviously he'd let the gripe session cloud his mind. This was an ops, he firmly reminded himself. And the woman he was gawking at was his partner.

He quickly got his mind on something else.

They walked through the master suite and into the bathroom. Their weapons and other assorted communications equipment were there; all the items they might need over the next few days. Agent Ingram had even hung some of their clothes and had placed their luggage in the adjoining dressing room.

Tessa turned on the shower full-blast and, without removing her underwear—something Riley was truly grateful for—stepped inside the steamy spray. Since there was a showerhead in each corner, and since the space was large enough to accommodate an NBA team, Riley got in, too, to save some time.

He kept his attention focused elsewhere—on the ornate mosaic tiles, on the beveled glass of the shower door they'd left open.

On anything but Tessa.

He was pretty sure she was doing the same thing. Well, she was until she shifted to her right and bumped into him. How that happened, he didn't know. After all, it wasn't as if they ran short of space. But it happened. Her slick, wet, right butt cheek swished against the front of his slick wet boxers.

Man, she couldn't have touched him in a worse place. That particular part of him was having a tough time accepting that showering with an attractive woman wasn't anything less than foreplay.

"Sorry," she mumbled.

"Me, too," he mumbled back.

She glanced over her shoulder at him. "Why are you sorry?" she whispered, her nearly silent words muffled even more by the shower.

"Believe me, you don't want to know."

He watched that register. Frowning, then scowling, and finally shrugging, she turned off the water. Tessa stepped out and snagged a couple of thick, white, terry-cloth robes from a nearby rack. She tossed him one.

"Start explaining," Riley demanded before he even caught the robe.

Thankfully she didn't ask for clarification. Riley was dead certain Tessa knew exactly what he meant. Well, hopefully she did. He didn't intend to discuss their shower and his reaction to it. Nope. It was time to settle some business.

"If I'd refused the insemination outright, Fletcher would have canceled everything." As if she'd declared war on it, Tessa latched onto her shoulder-length blond hair and squeezed it. Hard. The water snaked down her nearly naked shoulders and arms before she put on the bathrobe. Finally. "And you know it as well as I do."

"I don't know any such thing. But what I do know is that it didn't solve anything by you agreeing to a procedure you can't have."

She picked up a comb from the vanity and raked it through the tangles in her hair. "I'll figure a way around it."

"And if you can't?"

"I'll figure out a way, okay?" But this time her words weren't quite so calm or so quietly spoken.

"Oh, yeah. That's really convincing." Riley caught onto her arm and whirled her back around to face him. "Once we're inside that facility, Tessa, you might not be able to refuse it. Hear me? If you do, Fletcher might get suspicious and try to kill you."

Which couldn't happen. *It couldn't.* He refused to lose another partner. Just the thought of it turned his stomach.

"So, what are you saying? You want to call off the mission?" Tessa asked. That was obviously a rhetorical question since she didn't give him a chance to answer. "You want to let Fletcher walk because of a contingency that may or may not arise?"

"No. But I don't want you to get pregnant, either."

She paused. Mumbled something indistinguishable under her breath. And combed her hair again. "There *really* is little chance of that happening."

Just because she said it with such certainty, that didn't convince Riley. "If you're thinking about using some form of birth control, it's too risky. Lab tests would detect—"

"Trust me. It's not an issue."

He was about to say something along the lines of *I beg to differ,* but there was something in her tone that stopped him cold.

"This isn't about birth control, is it?" he asked cautiously.

"No." And that was all she said for several long moments. Tessa slowly put the comb back on the vanity, aligning it with the soaps and other bottles of cosmetics. "If you must know, I had endometriosis when I was a teenager. It's a problem with tissue growing where it shouldn't. I had surgery. But the damage had already been done."

Since he had no idea what to say to that, he just stood there and listened.

"I have slim-to-none odds of getting pregnant even under ideal circumstances," she continued. Not easily though. Her bottom lip trembled. Just a little. And her voice wavered slightly. It was more than enough for him to realize this was no well-healed wound. "So Fletcher's procedure poses no risk whatsoever. For once, Murphy's Law is on our side."

Ah, hell.

Riley thought about reaching for her. Maybe even a touch to her arm. Some kind of human contact to let her know he was here for her. It'd make him feel better, that was for sure, but he didn't think it'd do a thing to help Tessa.

"That's the nerve I hit," he mumbled.

Her gaze lifted, meeting his. "Excuse me?"

"In the limo when I was talking about people screwing around with Mother Nature to get a baby. Or not get one. I hit a nerve."

She dismissed that with a shrug.

Riley knew better.

There was no way to dismiss the pain in her eyes.

"It's old baggage," she mumbled. "A dream about recreating a childhood, *my childhood,* with the child of my own. A dream where mothers don't leave one day and never come back." Suddenly looking disgusted with herself, she cleared her throat. "The kind of dream that sends people into therapy."

Oh, yeah. Definitely wounds.

"The bottom line is, the only thing I've ever wanted more than being an SIU agent is a baby, and I can't have one. So, there. You know all my deep, dark secrets." She flexed her eyebrows. "Guess that means I'll kill you now."

Her attempt at humor didn't diffuse anything.

Riley disregarded his veto about touching her and slipped his arm around her. Before she could protest, or before he could change his mind, he hauled her to him. Right against him.

"Don't," Tessa said, already trying to break out of his grip.

Riley held on. "This isn't sexual, Tessa."

She pulled back and faced him. "It'd be safer if it were," she countered.

That was one hundred percent true.

Riley still didn't let go.

"Does your father know about your infertility?" he asked.

"Of course."

Okay. It took him a moment to get his teeth unclenched. "And he let you come on this mission anyway?"

This time she did step away from him. But Tessa didn't just put some distance between them, she stared at him with accusing eyes. "Don't blame him." She hitched her thumb against her chest. "I lied to you this morning. I did have a choice. But I wanted to do this. For Colette."

"And for him," Riley added.

Her mouth tightened. "Maybe."

"There's no maybe about it. You don't want dear old dad to have an unsolved case on his docket. Don't get me wrong. It's admirable, especially since clearing that case will mean getting Colette's murderer."

Still, this went above and beyond duty to father, to country. This was a side to Tessa Abbot that he wouldn't have thought existed.

A side that made him feel…

Riley refused to let the rest of that thought enter his head. There was no place for personal feelings here. Live and learn. He'd already made that mistake once.

"Don't you dare question my ability to do this mission," she snarled. Gone was the wavery voice and the uncertainty in her eyes. Now, this was a look he was familiar with. Agent Tessa Abbot, the gung-ho, pain-in-the-ass operative who put duty above all else.

The facade might have worked, too, if only moments earlier she hadn't given him a glimpse of her heart.

"No questions or doubts, Tessa. Because it's my guess you have enough of those for both of us."

Tessa would have almost certainly denied that if the phone on the vanity hadn't rung. She reached over and jabbed the speaker button. Her father's image appeared on the small screen attached to the phone.

"Is this a good time to talk?" John Abbot asked.

"It's safe," Tessa told him. She paused only long enough to take in a breath. Probably so she could give the briefing her own personal slant. "We have a rendezvous time with our suspect. Per his instructions, in three days we'll be taken to a clinic and then to another medical facility. Both are unspecified locations. By then, we're anticipating you'll have a way for us to transmit any information we might find."

"There'll be off-site video and audio-feed capabilities. That's as much as we can risk with Fletcher's security. And we'll have a secondary team follow you to the locations for surveillance and backup." Abbot paused. "We're not sure if this is a problem yet, but Fletcher might have dug a little deeper in your records than we originally thought."

That was not what Riley wanted to hear. "Are our covers intact?"

"Yes. From all indications, they are."

But it wasn't a hundred percent. Of course, in their business, nothing was.

"There are also some indications that Fletcher is setting up some thermal infrared equipment so he can scan the estate," Abbot added.

Definitely not good. Visual eavesdropping. And a royal pain because there'd be few breaks from deep cover. In other words, it would require Tessa and he to touch. A lot. Or, at least, they'd have to be close enough to each other so they could pretend to touch.

Yet one more concern to add to Riley's growing list of concerns.

"Until we've heard any indication to the contrary," Abbot went on, "things will proceed as planned. Let me emphasize—your mission is to locate and re-trieve evidence. According to Fletcher's profile, he'll probably keep detailed records in his personal com-puter or on surveillance tapes."

"You don't think he'll still have the tape of Co-lette's murder, do you?" Tessa asked.

"No. At least not at the clinic where he'll be tak-ing you. Elsewhere, perhaps. But it's possible Fletcher will mention Colette, and there'll be either a computer record or tape of that. He's an arrogant man who likes to boast about his…accomplishments. That arrogance will almost certainly help us bring him down."

Riley could only hope. And if Fletcher's arro-gance wasn't his Achilles' heel, then he'd find an-other way to get that evidence.

"Once you've completed the assignment," Abbot continued, "and we have the two of you out of the facility, then the FBI will move in and make the ac-tual arrest."

Riley would have preferred to cuff the doctor him-self, but he didn't mind passing that honor along to his fellow law enforcement officers. As long as they nailed Fletcher, it would be a successful mission.

Too bad there was an *if* that threatened the success.

Riley waited a couple of seconds to see if Tessa would complete the briefing, but it soon became ap-parent she'd decided to leave out a critical detail.

"Do you plan to mention that part about Phase One of Project Ideal Baby?" Riley asked her. "Or should I?"

That earned him another of her lethal glares. However, her glare relaxed significantly when she turned back to the screen to face her father.

"Our suspect indicated that he'd be performing a routine, nonanesthetized procedure on me when we arrive at the first location."

Man, talk about breezing right over the problem. "What Tessa's trying to sugarcoat is that the doctor wants to inseminate her before he takes us to the second location."

If her jaw tightened any more, she'd probably chip her pearly whites. "And what Riley and you both know is that there is no chance of my becoming pregnant. Without the insemination, we won't be able to get inside Fletcher's organization or gather evidence about the murders. In other words, our mission will fail."

"I don't want that any more than you do," Riley firmly reminded her. "But your father needs to know what you're up against. It's still a medical procedure. And even though I suspect Fletcher's whole operation is a scam, you have no idea what he might do to you, all under the guise of inseminating you. You'll be at his mercy, and believe me, I don't think you'll care for Fletcher's brand of mercy."

"Is the operation a scam?" Abbot questioned.

Tessa nodded.

So, she'd picked up on the inconsistencies, as well. No surprise there. She was smart and probably better versed in fertility issues than he was.

"Evade the insemination if possible," her father instructed. There wasn't any change in his tone to indicate he was even slightly concerned about his daughter's well-being. "If the suspect insists that it be done, then it's your call as to whether or not to continue the mission."

Your call. Translation? *You're a serious wuss if you wimp out because of an almost-nil risk.* Even if "almost nil" amounted to something significant because Fletcher would be able to do pretty much anything to her under the guise of a simple insemination.

Tessa wouldn't wimp out.

That full-steam-ahead, push-for-success mentality would have normally pleased Riley. But there wasn't much that was normal or pleasing about this. That said, it wouldn't stop him from doing this job, either.

So, the number-one solution was to avoid the insemination.

Somehow.

Even if it meant calling Fletcher and renegotiating the whole deal. Maybe he could convince the doctor that Tessa had a phobia about such things. After all, the Tates were supposed to be neurotic and self-absorbed, so he'd try to get some mileage out of that.

"Contact me with your situation report at 0800 to-morrow," Abbot concluded, and the screen went blank.

"How did you know Fletcher was running a scam?" she asked Riley when she clicked off the phone.

"Lucky guess." He waited a moment. "But yours probably wasn't a guess, huh?"

"Not really. Fletcher's procedure of flushing and then replanting an embryo is possible, though illegal in this country and most others. But the technology to genetically manipulate a human embryo doesn't exist. So I doubt he'd bother with the former when he can't do the latter."

Riley nodded. That was his theory, too. "So, ba-sically he just uses insemination to impregnate his clients and pretends to do his DNA manipulation thing. The women walk out of his facility with a lot less money than they had when they entered, and they're pregnant with babies they could have con-ceived the old-fashioned way."

He winced at his choice of words, but Tessa merely dodged his gaze and resumed combing her hair. "By the time the couples realize they don't have the *perfect child*," she said, "it'll be too late. Fletcher will have closed up his operation and skipped town."

Or else the couples would be so attached to the kids that perfection no longer mattered.

Riley kept that part to himself. And he didn't get

to renew the insemination argument, either, because there was a knock at the bathroom door.

"We have a visitor," Agent Ingram relayed through the closed door. "It's Dr. Fletcher. He's here."

Adrenaline slammed through Riley. Not good adrenaline, either. "What does he want?"

"He says there are some questions about your records and he needs to see you right away."

Great. Just great.

"Oh, and he's not alone," the agent added. "There are two men with him and both are carrying concealed weapons."

Riley cursed

So did Tessa.

And they both reached for their guns.

Chapter Four

"Where's Fletcher now?" Tessa cracked the door open and asked Ingram, who was waiting on the other side for further orders.

"I left him and his two *assistants* outside on the front veranda. I told them that I couldn't let them in until I got the okay from you."

Good. So, they weren't actually in the house. That was something at least.

If Fletcher had been let in, he could use the opportunity to plant some kind of listening device. That would precipitate a thorough scrub-down of the place. A scrub-down that would take hours for Riley and her to do. But even if that hadn't been an issue, Tessa was glad Fletcher was still outside. There was just something unnerving about being under the same roof as the murdering doctor, and she wanted to delay it until she was ready to face him.

"Stay out of sight," Riley instructed Ingram. "We'll be downstairs in a couple of minutes."

Her father's warning raced through her head. *Fletcher might have dug a little deeper in your records than we originally thought.*

If the doctor had found nothing, the fact that he was still looking wasn't a good sign. An equally bad sign was that he'd made an impromptu visit barely an hour after Riley and Tessa had left his office.

"You think Fletcher's suspicious?" Tessa asked, hurrying. She peeled off her bathrobe and grabbed her leather shoulder harness. Beside her, Riley did the same.

"Maybe. Or maybe this is just what he considers first-class service to his clients. Either way, stay alert."

Tessa had no plans to do otherwise. "What about our weapons? If Fletcher has his thermal scanning equipment up and running, he'll be able to see that we're armed."

"Possibly. But it won't necessarily be out of character for the Tates. Remember, they're paranoid about security. They'd probably consider Glocks and other 9 mm weapons to be proper accessories."

True. But it could also make Fletcher's suspicions about them skyrocket.

Together, they went into the dressing room. As the shower, it was easily large enough for several people, but Riley had a unique way of occupying space. Not his size, necessarily, since he wasn't overly muscular. It was just his presence. Even with the rush of adrenaline, even with her nerves zinging from Fletcher's unplanned visit, she noticed.

And she was sorry she had.

Tessa blamed it on that ridiculous heart-to-heart chat they'd had just minutes earlier. She'd said things to Riley she hadn't intended to say. Ever. To anyone. Things that could have easily dissolved barriers that were best left between them. Thankfully the mission and Fletcher's visit would put those barriers back in place. Because there was no room for personal feelings here.

Now, she only hoped her body understood that.

If not, she'd make it understand.

Tessa held on to that thought until she saw Riley's boxer shorts land on the floor, mere inches from her feet. The boxers were obviously damp from the shower. So was her own underwear. Since it would have been ridiculous not to change it, she made sure her back was to him before she peeled off her bra and panties.

"Are you okay?" Riley asked.

She risked glancing over her shoulder at him. Yep. He was naked. Well, almost. He was in the process of putting on another pair of boxers to cover his incredibly toned backside. On a scale of one to ten…well, there was no scale to rate it. Backsides such as his defied traditional ratings.

She forced her attention elsewhere. "Why wouldn't I be?" she countered.

Their gazes met. For just a few seconds. It was more than enough time for Tessa to grasp what Riley meant. And it wasn't her involuntary reaction to his backside. Judging from the sympathy in his eyes, they were right back to the one subject she didn't want to discuss.

"I'm fine," Tessa snapped.

Annoyed and irritated that Riley apparently thought she was some fragile creature to be protected, she riffled through her clothes and located a garnet-colored silk lounging set and a matching robe. There were other garments in the closet that were more fitting for visits with a doctor, but this particular outfit was bulky enough to conceal her shoulder holster.

In this case, that took priority over fashion.

If Fletcher wasn't running infrared scans over them at this very moment, then there was no reason to advertise that they were armed.

When she finished dressing, Tessa stepped into a pair of slippers and whirled around to face him. She wanted to settle this issue once and for all before they met with Fletcher.

"Let's get something straight, McDade. My infertility problems will have no effect on this mission."

He zipped up a pair of well-worn, loose jeans, slung a black T-shirt over his bare shoulder and adjusted the slide holster around his waist. It was a really bad time to notice that his chest and abs were as equally toned as his butt—and just as interesting.

She was losing it if she could think of his physical attributes at a time like this.

What was wrong with her? She'd never had this kind of reaction to a fellow operative during a mission. Heck, she couldn't remember the last time she'd felt this way toward *any* man.

"Did you hear me?" she asked because the silence was really starting to get to her. "There's no reason for you to keep asking if I'm okay."

Well, there was, in a way, but Tessa wasn't about to open up a discussion about her insane attraction to him.

Riley stared at her a moment. Then, two. Before he nodded. Not necessarily a nod of concurrence, but it was apparently enough to get them started toward the door so they could put the subject behind them.

Or so Tessa thought.

Riley slipped on his T-shirt. "I want you to stay back. Not because of your medical issues," he quickly added before she could object. "And not because I don't trust you. I do. But if Fletcher is on to us, if he's learned we're agents, then this might turn ugly. One of us needs to play backup."

Yes. In case Fletcher had become more than suspicious and was here to eliminate them. It wouldn't be a first. The SIU believed that Fletcher had already murdered several times to cover up his illegal activities, and he probably wouldn't hesitate to do it again.

"Okay," Tessa concurred. "I'll do backup."

Riley reached for the door but then stopped and looked at her. "This might be a good time to ask Fletcher again if there's an alternative to the initial insemination."

She huffed. Tessa couldn't help it. "Haven't we been through this?"

"No. *You've* been through it, and each time you've dismissed my concerns. This time, you'll listen. Either you find a way around the procedure, or I'll be right there in the room with you when he does it. Because I won't leave you alone with that man."

Tessa was about to remind him that she was an agent, capable of taking care of herself. But Riley would no doubt only remind her that Colette had felt the same way.

And it would be true.

"Nod if you agree," Riley insisted.

"And if I don't?" she fired back.

"Not an issue, because you're going to agree."

Since Tessa was tired and riled with the argument, and since they had to deal with Fletcher, she nodded.

However, this subject wasn't closed.

Riley studied her eyes, as if trying to determine if she were telling the truth. "All right. Let's do this."

They made their way down the stairs with Tessa lagging several steps behind him. Neither drew their weapons, but she eased her hand into her robe and onto her holster in case she had to get to the 9 mm handgun in a hurry.

When they reached the foyer, she spotted Agent Ingram in the formal dining room. He was just out of sight, tucked behind a large plant, but he could respond if necessary.

Tessa prayed it wouldn't be necessary.

If this turned into a battle for their lives, they might never get the proof of what Fletcher had done.

Riley gave her one last, cautioning glance, and Tessa ducked into the hall that led toward the kitchen. That way, she, too, would be out of sight but still close enough to react.

She hoped.

She held her breath while Riley opened the door.

Tessa heard them exchange friendly greetings, but Riley's hand stayed firmly planted on the slide holster at the back waist of his jeans.

"I need to see your wife," she heard Fletcher say. "Is she available?"

Even though Fletcher's request was somewhat abrupt, it was amicable enough, but there would have been no reason for him not to be. After all, if he'd come here to kill them, he wouldn't have wanted to do that outside in the open where there'd be potential witnesses. No, he would simply wait until he'd gained access.

"It's important," Fletcher added when Riley didn't respond right away.

"My wife and I were, uh, in the shower." Riley gave that plenty of carnal undertones. "We weren't expecting visitors this afternoon."

"Then, I'm sorry I disturbed you." Fletcher paused. "But as I said, this is important. We have to talk."

Okay. So, Fletcher wouldn't be easily put off, which meant it was decision time for her. Since Tessa didn't want this *important* matter to jeopardize the mission, she stepped out from her hiding place and motioned for Ingram to take over as backup.

"Darling, what's wrong?" she called so that Riley would know she was approaching.

Judging from the brief glower Riley gave her, this was not what he'd had in mind. Tessa ignored his expression, smiled lovingly at him, and walked closer.

The logistics weren't easy because she didn't want to block Riley from being able to reach his gun. So she ducked beneath his arm and moved to his left side. She planted a kiss on his cheek, hoping it would make the whole maneuver appear intimate rather than necessary.

"Dr. Fletcher," she said. Tessa tried to sound surprised to find him standing on the veranda. He was holding a folder and had tucked it beneath his arm, probably so he could shake hands with her. But Tessa didn't offer her hand for him to shake. She wasn't about to put herself at risk for the sake of civility. "What are you doing here?"

He flashed her one of those slick smiles. And dodged her question. "I've discovered a possible problem with your application. May I come in?"

Oh, mercy. This couldn't be good.

Riley and she exchanged glances, and both did their best to convey to Fletcher that they weren't happy with the intrusion on their showering fun. Still, if they didn't cooperate with Fletcher, he might just cancel the medical procedure.

Obviously, Riley came to the same conclusion. "Sure. Come in," he offered.

But once Fletcher was inside, Riley put up his hand to stop the two armed thugs from entering.

"Is there a problem?" Fletcher inquired. "The men are my assistants."

"My wife and I have security issues, as well," Riley gruffly explained. "We don't allow strangers on the premises."

After several snail-crawling moments, Fletcher nodded, as if he understood their concern, but the understanding didn't quite make it to his eyes. Tessa didn't think it was her imagination that the doctor was riled and even a little unnerved.

She knew how he felt.

Playing the part of the good hostess, she ushered Fletcher into the sitting room just off the foyer so they'd still be in visual range for Agent Ingram. Riley followed closely behind.

"I'll make this brief," Fletcher said. Gone was the thin smile he'd used to greet them. His expression was all-business when he took a seat in a saddle-brown chair next to the massive stone fireplace. "The nurse who examined you a few days ago mentioned that you had a scar just below your navel on your abdomen."

The laparoscopy scar from her endometriosis surgery. Since the nurse hadn't brought it up, Tessa had dismissed it as a nonissue. Obviously it was an issue if it had prompted Fletcher to come to the estate. Of course, his question probably wasn't the only reason for his visit. A simple phone call would have given him the answer.

Tessa explained the procedure she'd had nearly a decade earlier.

That part was true.

The rest was a lie.

She looked Fletcher straight in the eye and told him that the surgery had corrected her medical problem and that as far as she knew there was absolutely no reason she couldn't conceive a child.

Riley slipped his arm around her shoulder and eased her closer to him. A comforting gesture, but it served another purpose, as well. Especially when he added the kiss to her cheek. That kiss and the long, lingering gaze he gave her would hopefully convince Fletcher that Riley and she were eager to get back to their "shower."

"Well, I can see that my concerns weren't warranted," Fletcher said.

"Totally unwarranted," Riley agreed. He didn't even look at Fletcher but instead kept his hot gaze on her.

The silence that settled around them was uncomfortable. Fletcher finally stood. "Then I suppose I'll be going."

Riley and Tessa stood, as well, adjusting their positions so they'd be able to draw their weapons.

"Oh. I almost forgot." Fletcher stopped and turned around to face them. He took the large manila envelope that he'd tucked beneath his arm and dropped it onto the table in the foyer. "Testimonials from some of my other clients. I thought you'd like to read them."

"Thanks. But, Doc, I have to tell you, we don't need testimonials to convince us that you're the right man for the job. All we want is the perfect baby, and we believe you can make sure we get him."

If Fletcher was flattered by Riley's praise, he didn't show it. "I'll see you in three days," he said flatly, and strolled to the door.

Tessa didn't feel her muscles relax until the man was gone. She waited until his henchmen and he were off the veranda before she took out the detector wand from the table and started the search for monitoring devices. Because Fletcher hadn't actually touched either of them, a shower wouldn't be necessary.

Thank goodness.

She still had remaining effects from the last one.

Tessa retraced Fletcher's steps, moving the wand over the chair where he'd sat and along the floor where he'd walked. She even scanned the doorknob.

Nothing.

Until she got close to the manila envelope that Fletcher had left. The soft beeps said it all. It contained a monitoring device.

And that meant the doctor was indeed suspicious.

Riley motioned toward Ingram and the agent took the envelope and headed toward the back of the house. It wouldn't be removed from the premises or destroyed, because that would only heighten Fletcher's reservations. But the documents would be reviewed for possible evidence and the device would be contained in a specific area. A zone where Riley and she would have to maintain deep cover.

"You think Fletcher found something when he was doing all that digging into our records?" Tessa whispered.

Riley moved closer and put his mouth directly against her ear. In doing so, his body brushed against hers. "Could be. Something spooked him, that's for sure. I'll have the surveillance team keep a closer eye on him."

Ironic, since Fletcher would no doubt be doing the same thing to them.

"We've got three days to figure out what he really wants to do with us," Riley added, his breath touching her cheek. Not an entirely unpleasant experience.

Tessa took a step back.

So did Riley. He stared at her a moment, shook his head, mumbled some profanity, and generally looked disgusted with both of them. Tessa didn't ask why. She didn't want or need clarification.

Three days.

Not much time.

Yet in some ways, it was an eternity. She'd be spending that time in close quarters pretending that she was insanely attracted to her partner.

And that in itself was enough, more than enough.

But Tessa also had to deal with her ever-increasing awareness that the attraction she felt for Riley McDade wasn't nearly as much of a pretense as she wanted it to be.

Chapter Five

Riley stood in the doorway that separated the bedroom from the bathroom and took a deep breath.

It didn't help.

Of course, he'd need a lot more than a deep
breath to help him through the night. A shot of
whiskey, maybe.

But that seemed a lot to ask of mere alcohol.

Tessa was already in bed. Thankfully covered with
the thick, down comforter that was almost the same
gunmetal blue as her eyes. Beneath that cover, she
was wearing ivory-colored pj's. Not provocative
ones, either. Simple. Plain. Like her sensible underwear.

Well, almost.

When they'd been in the bathroom earlier, Riley
had accidentally brushed up against the arm of those
pj's and hadn't been overly pleased to realize they
were silk.

Yes. Silk.

It was one of his weaknesses when it came to women. Not his only one though, not by a long shot. His ultimate weakness was an obvious one. A blatant male fantasy of having an attractive woman waiting for him beneath the covers.

Or even on top of the covers.

The fantasy was less specific when it came to location.

The point was that an attractive woman be waiting for him. And they would do something about that waiting.

Soon, very soon, reality would take over and he'd have to face down that fantasy and join the silk-wearing Tessa in bed.

Riley reconsidered having that shot of whiskey.

"Everything okay?" Tessa sounded concerned.

"Why'd you ask?"

She made a shruglike gesture. "You look…uncomfortable."

Oh, he was uncomfortable, all right.

Among other things.

Too bad some of those other things included being aroused and wanting her. That was coupled with his rather vivid imagination of how it would feel to unwrap Tessa from that silk and kiss every inch of her body.

Man, he was one sick puppy.

The absolute last thing he should be thinking about was getting her naked and kissing her.

"That look doesn't have anything to do with Fletcher's little gift, does it?" she asked.

She was referring to the eavesdropping device that Fletcher had left them in the envelope. It had been neutralized as much as they could risk neutralizing it. Agent Ingram had put it in the kitchen, which was now a "deep-cover zone." No private conversations there. Just the facade of a happily married couple.

Which explained why Tessa and he hadn't made any trips to the kitchen.

They'd both obviously had enough of the loving conversations. But with Fletcher's people running possible thermal infrared scans of the estate, all zones were hot.

Well, from a visual standpoint anyway.

And that was the reason he'd have to share the bed with Tessa. Their paranoia about security might explain away their need to carry weapons to answer the door or their habit of banning certain visitors, but it'd be a bear to explain why a couple who couldn't keep their hands off each other required separate beds.

Tessa sat up and leaned forward to adjust the comforter that had bunched up around her feet. Not good. He got an unfortunate glimpse down the front of her baggy, silk top. He saw her bra.

Not sensible.

Not this. It was white lace. One of those little

why-bother garments that barely skimmed her nipples, which were doing an ample job of escaping.

Yet another of his weaknesses.

Until now, Riley hadn't realized he had so damn many of them.

He forced himself not to hope for a full-fledged nipple escape, but he had to override some ancient male DNA to do that. And he forced himself to look elsewhere. That also required him to override a few more things, including some truly bad suggestions that certain parts of his body were making.

"Just how good do you think Fletcher's thermal scanning equipment will be?" Tessa asked. Evidently she had the same concerns he did.

Well, some of his concerns.

She probably didn't have a clue what that white lace bra was doing to him.

Torture.

Pure torture.

"The equipment's probably very good." Riley moved out of the doorway and, while focusing on the lamp beside the bed, walked toward her. He also made a cursory glance out the window and saw nothing out of the ordinary. "Fletcher's not the type to use anything less than the best."

She considered that a moment and cursed softly. Riley couldn't help it, he laughed. Not from humor. But from the irony of the situation. Both had declared numerous times to each other and to their mission commander that playing the part of a loving couple wouldn't be a problem.

They'd apparently been a little too hasty with their declarations.

Even though Tessa and he didn't see eye-to-eye, they were still human and they had human responses. All the training in the world couldn't negate the fact that he was a man and she was a woman.

And there was that other part about her fulfilling several columns on a hypothetical fantasy checklist.

Riley finally got into bed. Fortunately it was a big bed. Probably a custom size to fit the huge scale of the room. That was an advantage. At least it would have been if Fletcher hadn't been using those thermal scanning measures.

She turned off the lamp next to the bed. However, it didn't plunge the bedroom into total darkness. The security lights around the perimeter of the estate were more than ample to supply them with enough illumination so that he could still see her.

"We should talk about this," she mumbled.

As long as it didn't involve white lace bras and escaping nipples, he was all up for a good talk.

"About?" he asked, just so he didn't make a fool of himself by mistaking what she meant by *this*.

She hesitated and out of the corner of his eye he could see she was actually doing some lip-nibbling.

It was no surprise to him that he found that erotic, as well. Of course, at the moment her breathing seemed erotic.

"How much will Fletcher be able to delineate in the scans?" she asked.

A lot.

But Riley pushed that aside and concentrated on what they could do about it.

"The closer we are to each other, the harder it'll be for him to differentiate exactly what we're doing. Our combined body heat will blur the lines, so to speak."

Of course, the closeness would likely blur other lines—personal and professional ones—but Riley kept that to himself, as well. No sense spelling out the obvious.

"Okay," Tessa said.

A second later she repeated it.

Taking a deep breath of her own, she reached out, latched onto his arm and got him moving in her direction, until they were literally side by side.

His arm touching her arm.

His leg touching hers.

Riley suddenly wished he'd brought a pair of sensible pj's with him instead of the thin, snug, navy boxers. If his instincts were right about this scenario, extra layers of fabric would come in handy.

So would a long, cold shower.

Maybe a dozen of them.

"Fletcher probably wouldn't be suspicious if we bypassed the sex tonight," Tessa said. It sounded as if she were trying to convince herself more than him. "After all, you did *the thing* in his clinic. Plus, there was the shower incident. Or, at least, Fletcher thinks there was a shower incident. We could probably maintain cover with a fake good-night kiss and some snuggling."

Riley had come to the same conclusion, but a fake kiss and snuggling still required some fairly close contact to make it believable.

Bracing himself, or rather trying to, he rolled to his side. So they were facing each other. And he planted his right hand on her pillow.

"This," Riley said, "will look like a kiss on a thermal scan."

He hoped.

He leaned in, until his mouth hovered over hers. Just several inches away. It was still plenty close enough for him to smell her toothpaste. Spearmint. He'd never considered that arousing, but for some reason, it was tonight.

Riley angled his head to one side, lingered a bit, then he changed the angle. Not drastically. Just enough to replicate a couple moving in rhythm to a kiss.

Following his lead, she did the same. In the milky light, he saw Tessa smile. A moment later a somewhat muffled chuckle joggled her chest. An unwelcome joggle since it sent her breasts brushing against his chest.

. But for some reason, that brushing didn't hold his attention for quite as long as he'd thought it would. It took Riley a moment to realize why her unusual response captivated him. It was the first time he'd ever seen her really smile.

Man, it was a winner.

She had dimples and, combined with the soft spattering of freckles over her nose, she looked carefree and innocent. Unfortunately her full, sensuous mouth wasn't congruent with that innocent image. That was no schoolgirl's mouth. Her mouth was made for long, hot, slow French kisses. Kisses that would last for hours. Kisses that Riley's body volunteered him to deliver.

It was obvious his body still had some really stupid ideas.

"What's so funny?" he asked, hoping it would get his mind off her mouth.

It didn't, of course

With her so close, nothing could do that.

Her smiled widened. "I had an incredibly bad image of what it would take for us to simulate having sex."

Oh, yeah.

He'd had some of those images, as well. But they

weren't exactly a laughing matter—especially since during the next two and a half days they'd almost certainly have to delve into that simulation a time or two.

Still, Riley couldn't help but smile. "I'll bet no one ever warned you about things like this when you first became an agent."

She shook her head, the movement nearly brushing the tip of her nose against his. Hardly a kiss.

But he felt his body react.

Riley could hear his heartbeat start to pound in his ears. And for some insane reason, the cadence of his heartbeat began to sound like a pagan drum.

Urging him on.

Urging him to do something they'd both certainly regret.

"This is a first for me," Tessa answered, still smiling. "Usually I'm stuck in some surveillance van—alone."

He watched the words form on her mouth. Saw her smile widen, causing her dimples to flash again. And all he could think about was tasting that smile.

Tasting *her.*

"I'm sorry," she whispered. The smile faded. Just like that, it was gone, and Riley felt the loss as if someone had stripped away all the warmth in the room. "That must have made you think about Colette."

No.

His thoughts hadn't been of Colette.

But of Tessa.

And that was a huge problem.

Because thoughts like that could be fatal. He wasn't about to risk Tessa's life because he couldn't keep focused on the mission.

The light mood evaporated as quickly as it had come, and Riley moved away from her, dropping back onto the mattress so they were side by side. It was far safer than staring into her crisp blue eyes and pondering the nuances of her mouth and her smile.

"I know this can't be easy for you," she said. "It has to bring back the memories."

Riley hesitated a moment until he was sure he had control of his voice. "It probably brings them back for you, too."

"Yes."

Different images replaced the carnal thoughts. Not new images, though. The same ones of Colette that had tormented him for two years. "It's amazing how one person can effect so many lives."

Tessa made a sound of agreement. "That's why it's so important to prove Fletcher killed her."

It was important for a lot of reasons. "And when that happens, your father's record will be spotless again and he'll no doubt get that promotion to department chief. You'll probably get your promotion, too."

"That's not what I meant."

"I know." Riley turned his head to look at her and

saw the semiscowl that his remark had put on her face. Even though it wasn't an especially attractive expression, he preferred it to the smile.

It was safer.

A lot safer.

"All I'm saying is that closing out this case will benefit everyone," he clarified.

Especially him.

It couldn't bring back Colette. It wouldn't bring back the love or the life they'd planned together. But maybe if he managed to get justice for her, he'd be able to live with what had happened.

Maybe.

Because what he'd been doing for the past two years didn't really constitute living.

"I know you think I'm doing all of this for my father," he heard her say. "But you're wrong."

Riley had a pang of guilt and was sorry he'd tossed that remark at her. "You don't have to defend your relationship with your father."

"I'm not defending it. It's just…well, it's just I know people in SIU talk. And I hear what they say behind my back. He's a tough man. Always has been. But he raised me on his own after my mom left us when I was barely eight. It wasn't easy for him to take care of me. Not with the hours he was putting in at work. He could have pawned me off on some relative, but he didn't. He made sacrifices in his career, and if it weren't for all that time he spent with me, he would have made chief by now."

And whether Tessa realized it or not, she was defending him. She was also giving Riley a glimpse of what made her tick.

Guilt.

A whole boatload of it.

An emotion he totally understood.

"You're a good agent," Riley assured her. "You don't need to prove anything. Not to your father. Not to others. Not even to me."

She didn't respond. Not so much as a huff or a sound to indicate she was thinking about that. And the silence closed in around them.

"I guess you could say I joined the agency because of my father," Riley said to fill that silent void. And maybe there was another reason. After all, Tessa had shared an important piece of herself with him. Of course, that didn't mean he had to reciprocate, but Riley found himself doing it, anyway.

"My father's career army," he continued. "He's retired now, but he was once in special ops—Delta Force. The man has two Purple Hearts. *Two.* And he refuses to even acknowledge them because he says they're just reminders that he didn't duck fast enough."

Tessa made a sound of amusement. "So why didn't you join the army?"

"Because of that whole living-in-his-shadow thing. I wanted a different benchmark to gauge what I accomplished in life." And somehow they were right back to that driving force—guilt. Because his own benchmark hadn't done a thing to stop him from failing.

"What did your parents think of Colette?" she asked.

Maybe because she sensed what he was feeling. No surprise there. He wasn't good at hiding the pain from Colette's death. He wasn't sure he *wanted* to be good at that.

"My folks never met her." Yet another of the regrets in his life. "Colette and I had been seeing each other only about four months when we decided to get married. I kept meaning to drive down to Richmond with her so she could meet them. But it didn't happen. You know the drill—work got in the way."

"But they would have loved her," Tessa concluded.

"Yeah. My mom especially." He hoped he hadn't thoroughly depressed Tessa with that comment. He sure as heck was depressing himself. "How about you? Ever brought a guy home to meet your dad?"

"Once." She paused and idly snuggled closer. She also, idly, brushed her leg against his. That touch, that reminder that she was a woman, didn't cure his depression, but it fired his fantasies all over again. "It was nearly ten years ago. The guy was in law school and I was a sophomore in college. I was barely nineteen and thought I was in love."

"But you weren't?"

She shook her head, creating yet another interesting touch scenario where her cheek swished against his. Riley felt his groin tighten. "It was lust," she insisted.

Riley read between the lines, once he got past an initial kick of jealousy. Sheez. Where had that come from? "And this law-school jerk broke your heart?"

Another nod. Another swish. "I guess I didn't duck fast enough."

Yeah.

He understood that, too.

Everything was suddenly so quiet. Too quiet. The sound of the phone ringing shot through the room. Not the secure phone in the bathroom, either, but the one next to the bed. Riley checked the clock. Just past midnight.

Hardly the time for a social call.

Since that meant something had probably gone wrong, Riley got out of bed and pressed the speaker button on the phone.

"I hope I didn't wake you," Fletcher greeted.

Even though Riley had already anticipated that it would be the doctor, hearing his voice sent his adrenaline level through the roof.

"We were in bed," Riley informed him. "It's late."

"Yes, it is. But I trust it's not too late for us to get started."

Okay. That didn't help the adrenaline. Obviously it had the same effect on Tessa. She threw back the covers and joined Riley on his side of the bed so they were both staring at the phone.

"What do you mean?" Riley asked Fletcher.

"Within the next two minutes, a limo should be pulling up in front of the estate. The driver is Beatrice. Since you've already met her, I trust you won't consider her a stranger. I mean, I know your concerns about security."

And those concerns had quadrupled with this particular call. "What's this all about, Doc?"

"Beatrice will drive you and your wife to a clinic where I'll be doing the initial procedure."

Hell.

"Now?" Tessa questioned.

"Now," Fletcher quickly assured her.

Oh, man. The timing sucked. The mission director probably didn't have all the surveillance measures in place. Not this soon. But Riley hoped that the SIU had anticipated that Fletcher would do the unpredictable and that Tessa and he would at least need some backup.

"Why so soon?" Riley demanded, trying to keep his tone civil. Not easy to do considering their best-laid plans were starting to crumble.

While he waited for Fletcher to respond, Riley motioned for Tessa to go into the bathroom. She'd need to use the phone in there to call headquarters to alert them about the apparent change in plans. She also needed to warn Agent Ingram, who was probably asleep in one of the rooms downstairs.

Tessa obviously understood what had to be done and she hurried into the other room and closed the door so that the doctor wouldn't be able to hear her conversation. Of course, it might still tip off Fletcher if he was in the process of a thermal scan, but there wasn't much Riley could do about that now. Hopefully, it would seem as if Tessa were merely listening in on the other phone.

"I have my own security concerns," Fletcher answered. "And I prefer to keep things a little unpredictable."

This was like déjà vu. Fletcher had done the unpredictable the day Colette died.

"Can't this wait until morning?" Riley snatched up his jeans and T-shirt and slipped them on.

"The timing isn't negotiable," Fletcher answered. "You see, I reevaluated the ovulation information that your wife gave to my medical staff, and I realized I'd seriously miscalculated. We have to move up the procedure if we want to assure success. And you do want this to succeed, don't you?"

Riley silently cursed. This wasn't part of some

reevaluation but was no doubt Fletcher's plan all along so he'd have the element of surprise.

And it had worked.

Heaven help them, it had worked.

"Ah, I understand Beatrice is at the estate now," the doctor continued. Riley glanced out the window and confirmed that. A black limo had just pulled to a stop right in front of the door. "Take nothing with you to the clinic. *Nothing.* And that includes phones and pagers. Everything you need will be provided."

"I'm not prepared with the monies we discussed this afternoon, given that you had said it would be three days," Riley said, hoping to change Fletcher's plans.

"Understandable. You can make payment arrangements tomorrow via telephone from the clinic. I'm sure it can all be taken care of before the final medical procedure takes place."

Riley knew there was no argument he could make that would delay this. With Fletcher's penchant for secrecy and security, failure to leave now would almost certainly close down the mission.

Tessa came out of the bathroom and since they couldn't really talk, he tried to read her expression.

Not exactly optimistic.

"Can you stall him?" she mouthed.

Riley shook his head.

"You have to leave now," Fletcher said, as if he knew they were hesitating. And he probably did.

"I'm afraid I must insist. In fact, Beatrice is making her way to your door."

It was decision time and Riley knew there was only one choice Tessa and he could make.

They had to go.

"Put on your shoes," he instructed Tessa.

Riley did the same. When she sat next to him on the bed, she opened her hand so that he could see the watch. It was a nifty piece of equipment that she'd snagged from the equipment bag in the bathroom. A transmitter and receiver that could disrupt signals and even in some cases act as a homing device. He slipped it onto his wrist.

Tessa pointed to her own wrist to show Riley that she, too, was wearing a transmitter. It might come in handy if his failed, but it wouldn't do a thing to keep them alive. And since they couldn't risk carrying in a weapon, it meant they had to rely on their training and instincts.

Riley prayed that was enough. And while he was at it, he prayed that he was doing the right thing.

"Your wait is almost over," Fletcher continued, his voice both calculating and cheerful at the same time. "I'm preparing for the insemination now. In less than an hour, you two will be well on your way to having the perfect baby."

Oh, hell.

An hour.

Much too soon.

But that didn't matter. There was nothing they could do about it.

Riley clicked off the phone, took Tessa by the hand and started for the door.

Chapter Six

The clinic was sterile.

That was Tessa's first reaction to the facility where Beatrice had driven them. Odd, since it was supposed to be a haven for conception. Her opinion of the place didn't change, either, when Dr. Fletcher took Riley and her into the examination room.

Sterile, also.

Bare, milk-white walls. Cold, chalky tiles on the floor. Odorless. And with the exception of Fletcher, Beatrice and them, the building was seemingly deserted. Tessa neither saw nor heard anyone, even though she was certain that Fletcher's security goons were nearby.

The doctor wasted no time with the procedure. In less than five minutes after they arrived, he had her changed into a hospital-style dressing gown. And only seconds after that, she was on the examination table while he performed the insemination.

During the whole ordeal, Riley stayed with her, his hand clutching hers, their gazes fastened to each other. It would no doubt appear intimate and loving to an observer.

It wasn't.

By keeping his attention focused solely on her, he was actually giving her the only measure of privacy that she could have in this situation.

Tessa divided her attention between making sure Fletcher didn't do anything unexpected—she'd had enough surprises already—and concentrating on figuring out where the heck they were.

Riley was no doubt doing the same.

The windows had been blackened in the limo, and their watches had stopped transmitting. Even though Tessa had been unable to see where Beatrice was taking them, she'd kept careful count of the turns. The trip had taken less than a hour. Of course, it probably wasn't the most direct route, and the woman had no doubt been instructed to make sure she wasn't being followed.

And she very well might not have been.

That call Tessa had made to headquarters right before they'd left the estate had sent her father scrambling to assemble a surveillance team. Agent Chris Ingram would have followed the limo, of course. But he might not have been able to tail Beatrice for long.

So, there was only about a fifty-fifty chance that anyone in SIU knew their exact location. And even if they did, they might not be able to intercede if trouble started.

Tessa couldn't help but be concerned about that.

Because this had the potential of becoming a worst-case scenario.

Still, she had to concentrate on the parts of the mission that had succeeded. They were inside the clinic. All was seemingly going well. And with luck, the ops would proceed as planned.

But, mercy, she hated to rely on luck.

"All done," she heard Fletcher say. He pulled down his green surgical mask and walked around the examination table so he could face them. He gave her a comforting pat on the arm that nearly made her skin crawl. "You'll need to rest here for a few minutes, then I'll move you two to a room so you can get some sleep. I suspect you're tired."

A massive understatement. It was nearly two in the morning and she'd been up nearly twenty-four straight hours. And it would be heaven knew when before she got any real rest. Now that Phase One of Project Ideal Baby was finished, they had to prepare for the move to the other facility.

Of course, with Fletcher's penchant for surprises, there could be no second facility. Either way, here or there, Riley and she had to do whatever was necessary to search the place, then figure out how to tap into Fletcher's records to see if he'd left any incriminating evidence behind.

"I'll be right back," Fletcher said. "I need to check on a few things."

It was a welcome reprieve. The moment the doctor was out of the room, Riley faked a yawn and laid his head next to hers.

"Are you okay?" he asked.

"Yes. It wasn't painful at all." Definitely not as difficult as some of the procedures she'd endured when she was a teenager.

Riley readjusted his position, just slightly, but in doing so, he moved his hands between them. He raked his thumb over the base of his watch.

"Good, just touching base," he whispered.

This time the words weren't meant for her but for anyone at SIU headquarters who might be monitoring their equipment. Riley leaned in close and cupped her neck, then gently nuzzled her cheek with his own. His watch lay directly beneath both their ears. And they waited.

Praying that someone was indeed monitoring.

"Can you give us your location?" an almost-silent response came several seconds later.

Riley's gaze met hers for a mutual mental groan of relief. They had communication. That was the good news. The not-so-good news was that apparently SIU didn't know where they were, or the person wouldn't have asked that question.

"Thirty minutes, south southeast of Dallas," Tessa whispered, turning her cheek into Riley's hand. "Rural. One-story brick surrounded by woods."

Riley concurred with a mumbled yes that he covered by kissing her on the cheek. They'd both no doubt estimated distances, but with little visual, it was difficult to pinpoint where they'd been taken.

"We've got a general direction off your signal. We'll keep searching," the person assured them before he ended the transmission.

With luck, the search might be productive. However, they couldn't rely on it.

Riley moved his thumb from his watch, ending the connection they had with SIU, and put his mouth to her ear again. "Are you ready for a little recon?"

She smiled, as if he'd just whispered a sweet nothing instead of a cue for them to begin their search.

Tessa threw off the white cotton sheet that Fletcher had used to cover the lower half of her body. The gown only went to midthigh and, without her underwear, she felt more than a little exposed. She took the time to put back on her panties while Riley pretended to occupy himself with another yawn and a stretch.

When she'd finished dressing, Riley looped his arm around her waist and they went to door. Tessa expected to see Fletcher or a guard standing there, but they had the doorway and the hall to themselves.

They didn't walk toward the entrance where Beatrice had ushered them into the building. Instead, Riley and she went in the opposite direction. Down a corridor with two doors.

Both closed.

Riley tested the first one and found it unlocked. It appeared to be another examining room similar to the one they'd just left. Unfortunately there were no windows and no sounds of activity anywhere outside the building to give them a clue about their location.

Riley shut the door and led them to the next one. It was an office, complete with a laptop computer sitting on top of a desk. Judging from the artwork and the expensive rug, it was Fletcher's office.

They stepped just inside and scanned the place for cameras or other surveillance equipment. None visible.

Which meant nothing.

"Should we?" Tessa whispered.

He nodded. "You go, I'll stay." Then, in a normal level voice that was for the benefit of anyone monitoring them, Riley added, "Darling, I'm sure no one will mind if you check your e-mail."

Tessa didn't waste another second. But she didn't hurry, either. She tried to make it seem as if she were only mildly curious about the computer. That way, if they were being observed, she could explain that she was indeed doing something as innocuous as checking her e-mail.

Tessa booted up and did a quick scan through the files to see if there was something obvious. Not that she expected to see a file labeled with Colette's name, but she did check for hidden files.

And she found nearly a dozen.

Dr. Barton Fletcher was listed as the author in the file summary in the first file she checked. Tessa slid her gaze down to the comments section. Nothing in the first. Or the second. But then she finally spotted a familiar name in the third file summary.

Patient Number 823: Ellen Carmichael.

The cover name that Colette had been using when she was murdered.

Tessa's heart jumped to her throat. This was perhaps the very evidence they'd been searching for.

Unfortunately the file was huge and would take her more than a few minutes to examine. Worse, if she opened it, Fletcher would learn that it had been accessed and probably move or even delete it.

That couldn't happen.

They were too close to let the evidence get away from them now.

"What are you doing in there?" she heard someone ask.

Not Fletcher.

But Beatrice.

"My wife wanted to check her e-mail," Riley quickly volunteered.

He eased just inside the door, blocking Beatrice's view of the room. It was only a temporary measure though, and Tessa knew it. Beatrice would do whatever it took to get inside.

Tessa managed to get the computer closed down just seconds before Beatrice muscled her way past Riley, her gaze snaring Tessa right away. The woman lacked some of the subtly of her slick boss because she slipped her hand inside her jacket and Tessa's body went on full alert. Still, she forced herself not to overreact. The situation was salvageable.

She only hoped Beatrice cooperated with that theory.

Beatrice's mouth tightened. "I'm afraid you're not allowed in here."

"Is there a problem?" This time, it was Fletcher. He, too, appeared in the doorway, and judging from his disdainful expression, the gathering wasn't social.

"There's no problem," Tessa assured him. "We were just out for a little walk, and I thought it'd be a good time to check my e-mail. Especially since none of our friends know where we are. I had scheduled coffee with a friend tomorrow. I was afraid they'd get worried when they didn't hear from me and try to contact…someone."

And Tessa left it at that. "Someone" in this case would be the authorities. Maybe that would justify her actions.

Maybe.

Fletcher's attention slid from her to the computer. His attention lingered there just long enough to cause her stomach and chest to tighten. "My office and the other examining rooms are off-limits," he reprimanded. "Patient confidentiality. I'm sure you understand."

Tessa nodded and tried to look embarrassed at her faux pas. "Of course."

"Your room is ready," Fletcher finally said. "It's not as accommodating as the estate, but I believe you'll find everything you need." He turned as if to leave but then stopped. "Oh, and once you're inside the room, your door will be locked. Don't let that alarm you. It's simply a security precaution."

Riley propped his hands on his hips. "A security precaution?" He shook his head. "I don't like locked doors. I have this problem with claustrophobia."

"Then perhaps I can give you a sedative or something. Because I'm afraid there's no other option, Mr. Tate. The door will remain locked until morning. And please don't try to tamper with it, either. If the guards see you wandering around the hall, they might mistake you for an intruder and will respond accordingly."

Tessa truly didn't care for that term, "accordingly."

"Is this necessary?" she demanded. "We're your patients not your prisoners."

Fletcher dismissed her with a sharp glance. "The security's necessary. As is the guard who'll be posted outside your door. As I mentioned in Dallas, there are those who object to what I do. We must all be careful."

And with that not so veiled threat, Fletcher turned and walked away.

IT'D BEEN A TOUGH day and Tessa was positive it wasn't about to get easier.

After they'd been locked in their so-called guest suite, one with an observation window on the door and a guard posted just outside, Riley and she dressed for bed.

In the same bedroom, of course.

In fact, dressing and undressing in front of each other was becoming a common occurrence on this mission. Not that she was sneaking looks or anything like that, but there was a weird kind of intimacy that happened when you stripped down in front of a man. And that intimacy happened even if it wasn't supposed to happen.

Such as now, for instance.

Even though Tessa was doing everything humanly possible not to watch Riley, she heard his "issued" pajama bottoms whisper over his skin when he pulled them on. A sound that for some strange reason really revved up her body. A revving she would ignore because she'd been trained to put duty first and all else second.

Her involuntary physical reaction would definitely come in second tonight.

Definitely.

Tessa repeated that to herself.

She finished putting on her nightgown and slid into bed. Riley flicked off the lights and joined her. Like the room at the estate, the lack of overhead lights didn't plunge them into total darkness. The fluorescent lights in the hall were still on and enough seeped through the observation window to give them adequate illumination.

Not a welcome amenity, either. If she could see Riley, then that meant Fletcher could see them.

Of course, that might not even be necessary if the man was still monitoring them with thermal infrared equipment, as well. And he probably was.

Wondering how they were going to carry on a conversation about what she'd found in the computer files, she glanced at Riley, but it didn't stay a glance exactly. It turned into a full stare.

Oh, mercy.

What had she done to deserve this?

And better yet, how was she going to deal with these unwanted sensations simmering inside her? All right. So they weren't exactly simmering anymore. Those sensations had started to boil.

Riley's hair was tousled. Again. Not unkempt. And more than a little attention-getting. It was a stark contrast against the white pillow. As was his skin. Something else to capture her attention. Tessa knew from reading his dossier that his mother was Italian. His paternal grandfather, a born-and-bred Scot. Riley had inherited his mother's Mediterranean-olive skin. His grandfather's Highlander attitude.

Simply put, he was hot.

Not drop-dead gorgeous. And definitely no pretty boy. She wouldn't have been attracted to him if he had been.

And there was no denying it—she was attracted.

It didn't matter, of course. Nothing would come of it. At a minimum, a personal involvement during an ops would seriously violate regs. But that wasn't the only reason. As did Riley, she needed to stay focused, to close out this mission and then see what she could do about clearing her father's name and getting that promotion.

Besides, Riley had his own issues to deal with. He was still grieving for Colette. In fact, Tessa suspected he'd been thinking about Colette when they were at the estate. That would explain his physical reaction to her. That, and the old stand-by excuses: adrenaline and the intimacy created by close proximity.

And Tessa was almost certain she believed that.
Almost.

Riley moved closer to her, bringing with him the scent of the tropical-smelling soap that had been in the shower. Another "oh, mercy" moment.

"We're probably being watched," she whispered. Not that it would come as a surprise to him, but she thought it best if she tried to concentrate on the mission.

"Guaranteed. I think the camera's behind the mirror over the dresser."

She nodded. "What about eavesdropping equipment?"

"The detector on my watch located some kind of monitoring equipment in this room, but judging from the weak signal, it's probably only strong enough to pick up sounds louder than a whisper."

Tessa hoped that was true.

But just in case, they needed to be careful about what they said. Not easy. Because they had a lot to say to each other. For one thing, they needed to figure out what their next move was going to be.

That computer check had cost them dearly, and Fletcher wouldn't let down his guard again anytime soon. Still, they had to figure out a way to get back in there.

Riley turned to his side and faced her. "I never did ask—were you able to access your e-mail?" he said out loud.

"No." Also said out loud. Tessa moved closer to him and gave him one of those air kisses. "I wonder why Dr. Fletcher is so concerned about security?"

Riley took a few moments as if considering that. "There are a lot of jealous people out there, darling. People who might try to stop us from getting our baby."

In the dusky light, she saw him glance in the direction of the camera. She also saw the debate he was having with himself about what to say.

Or how loudly they could get away with saying it.

He reached for her. Curving his arm around her waist, he slid her closer, turned and eased on top of her. But that wasn't all he did.

Oh, no.

He aligned their bodies in the best way possible to convince Fletcher that they were in the throes of foreplay and not having a crucial conversation about possible incriminating evidence.

Of course, even though this was a charade, their body alignment was torture. As were the fake kisses that Riley aimed at her. Yes, they were indeed pretend, but since his warm breath landed on her mouth, they felt very much like the real thing.

It took more than a few seconds for Tessa to tamp down her own breathing so she wouldn't sound as if she were on the verge of an asthma attack.

"Do we seem like missionary-position people to

you?" Riley asked, obviously hoping to interject some humor into a situation that needed some.

Tessa smothered a laugh by clamping her teeth over her bottom lip for a few seconds. "I wouldn't know. It's been well over a year since I've experienced any position, missionary or otherwise." Sheez. She shook her head. "And why I just said that, I'll never know."

Now it was his turn to chuckle. "It's been a while for me, too. Besides, even if we're not supposed to be the conventional type, tonight we can blame our lack of creativity on fatigue."

And therein was a major problem. Fatigue wasn't helping in her case. In fact, it was doing just the opposite. The thick haze in her head was clouding the fact that this was all for show and tell.

Not good.

Because a few moments of levity and embarrassing confessions didn't soften what she had to say.

"There are about a dozen hidden files in Fletcher's computer," Tessa whispered. She also paused. "One of them mentions Ellen Carmichael."

She felt him freeze. It was no doubt a name he recognized instantly. One that would be forever part of his memory.

And not a good memory, either.

"That was the cover name Colette used for her last case," he mumbled.

"Yes. The file might not contain anything useful though," Tessa explained, her voice with hardly any sound. "But it's large and it's a start."

And it just might be the very thing that would make all of this worthwhile.

"Are you okay?" she asked.

Riley dodged the question. "What else did you find?"

"Other files. They all seem to be connected to the Ideal Baby project, but I won't know what's in them until I can go through each one."

"You need a way to copy them so the SIU techs can study each file." Riley dipped his head down and kissed her. Not an air kiss and not her mouth. It landed on her cheek, but it was close enough so that it would appear like a legitimate full-blown kiss. And they moved, adjusted and otherwise simulated the throes of passion-inducing foreplay so they could mask a conversation with the sound of the rustling cover. "Fletcher might have a disk we could use."

Yes. But that would take time to find. Time to copy. And then there was the whole issue of getting such a disk out of here. Fletcher wouldn't hesitate to search them, under the guise of maintaining security.

Heck, he wouldn't hesitate to kill them, either.

Riley worked his fingers through her hair, pressed another kiss on her neck.

Tessa sucked in her breath.

"Not there," she mumbled, adding a soft groan. "That doesn't feel fake."

"Welcome to the club," he grumbled right back at her.

That brought Tessa's gaze searching for his. And she found it. For one of those long, lingering looks like the ones that passed between lovers. Or between two people who were on the verge of becoming lovers.

Riley shook his head. "This can't happen between us, understand?"

"Believe me, I know."

He cursed and rustled the cover some more. "Oh, saying that helped a lot. And just in case you didn't catch the sarcasm, I'm not even close to being serious."

"It's the…fatigue." Best not to suggest the adrenaline anymore. She'd already worn out that particular excuse.

Riley stared down at her. "Right. And it has nothing to do with you being an attractive, half-naked woman who just happens to be lying beneath me with her leg thrown over my butt."

She moved her leg.

"I'm not half-naked," she insisted.

"Close enough. My mind is more than willing to fill in the blanks."

Her lips quivered, fighting back a smile. She lost that fight.

"Ah, hell," Riley whispered. "This was so much easier when we were discussing disks and files."

He was right.

But he still leaned in even closer. So did she. Why, she didn't know. It was stupid, and what they were apparently about to do would up that stupidity several dozen notches.

Yet she didn't stop him.

She didn't stop herself.

Riley touched his mouth to hers. Just a touch. It barely qualified as a kiss. Barely.

And that was truly scary, because it packed a wallop.

He groaned softly. A rich, male sound that curled around her, clouding her mind even more than it already was. Well, clouding it in some ways. In other ways, that sound seemed to hone every nerve, every sensation.

Everything.

Tessa couldn't fall for him. She just couldn't. It would start another nightmare. One where one of them, or both, would lose focus.

"We need to finish this," Tessa whispered. Not easily. Her voice was strained and uneven. "I mean, not finish this *this*. But the show we started."

"Yeah. The show." And Riley repeated it while he levered himself up slightly so he would appear to be having sex with his wife.

Unfortunately, Riley and she didn't have the fake rhythm part down pat because she adjusted her legs just as he lowered for what would be a thrust.

No "air" thrust as he'd probably planned. No air anything. It was complete contact, and she went from the I'm-fighting-this, hurry-up stage to being fully aroused.

Not exactly the response she'd wanted.

But it was impossible to stop.

And for Riley, impossible to hide.

Worse, his erection pushed right against the soft intimate folds of her body. It didn't matter that he had on his pj bottoms and that she was wearing panties and a gown. The sensation was practically blinding. Judging from Riley's not-so-soft grunt, it was the same for him.

Tessa fought with her breath. Riley fought with his. And she tried to stay perfectly still, hoping to lessen the effect.

Not that it was possible to do that.

But the stillness allowed her a chance to battle some of those primitive demands that were begging her to take him. Right then, right there. And to heck with the consequences.

"Brace yourself," he mumbled.

Another thrust. Then, another. With each one, her heartbeat pounded in her ears. Her body softened. And begged.

Mercy, did it beg.

Every inch of her wanted every inch of him.

One last thrust—but just because it was the last, it didn't mean it wasn't as effective as the others. Mainly because he had to collapse on top of her, which put his erection in the one general area she truly wanted it to be.

"Sorry," he mumbled.

"It's the fatigue," she whispered back.

"So you've said."

It was bull, of course, and both of them knew it. To the best of her knowledge, fatigue had never caused her to come close to having an accidental orgasm. No. Riley had caused that.

"In an hour I'll check the hall for the guard," he whispered. "If he's gone, we can get back into Fletcher's office. In the meantime, you get some sleep. I'll take first watch."

She didn't argue. She couldn't. Tessa was still having trouble speaking. "Wake me in a half hour," she finally managed to say.

After a few unbearable seconds, where he was obviously pretending to catch his breath from the fake—and the real—exertion, Riley rolled off her and landed on his back. Probably because it was expected of a loving husband, he snuggled against her.

Worse, he fit.

She fit, too.

As if she belonged there. There, next to him. Wrapped in his arms.

For a lot of reasons—and that *fit* was definitely one of them—Tessa knew it was going to be a heck of a long night.

Chapter Seven

Riley stared up at the ceiling and listened for any activity both inside or outside the clinic. The only thing he heard, however, was the rhythmic rise and fall of Tessa's breathing.

For some reason, it was calming.

Unlike everything else.

He had a sickening feeling that everything was on the brink of chaos.

It was nearly 6:00 a.m. Almost time to do another search of the hall to see if it was clear. So far, it hadn't been. Either Tessa or he had checked every couple of hours, on the pretense of using the bathroom or getting a drink of water, and each time they'd seen two armed guards, one posted at each end of the hall.

Not good.

Fletcher was perhaps on to them, or else the double guards were just a reflection of his paranoia about security. Either way, it meant Tessa and he were literally under house arrest. If they challenged the guards, then it would possibly result in a fight for their lives. At a minimum, Fletcher would almost certainly ask them to leave.

So they were in the wait-and-see mode.

Not exactly a comforting place to be.

Riley shifted slightly, facing Tessa. A huge mistake. Just the sight of her face caused emotions and feelings to swell inside him. Things he no longer thought himself capable of feeling. Feelings that went well past basic attraction.

He silently cursed.

Hell, hadn't he learned anything from that fatal mission with Colette?

Apparently not.

He reached out and pushed a lock of Tessa's dark blond hair from her forehead. She stirred, a little, and peeked out at him. Man, even blurry with sleep, those eyes were something else.

As if he needed anything else about Tessa Abbot to be memorable.

"Go back to sleep," he whispered. "It's not time yet."

She gave a groggy nod and closed her eyes.

Riley was thankful for the temporary solitude. Not that he thought solitude could help him come to terms with whatever this was that was happening between them. There were so many reasons why there shouldn't be an attraction, and Riley mentally went through them. Regulations. The mission. The fact that neither had the time or probably the inclination for a personal relationship or commitment. And Colette. He'd gone this route before and it had ended in disaster.

Going through those reasons didn't undo anything.

But it did help him come up with a way to neutralize some of the effects.

For one thing, there'd be no more fake kisses. No more fake sex. No intimacy, either fake or otherwise. He'd feign an illness, a sore throat maybe. Anything that would explain why he was no longer touching his *wife*.

Of course, that begged the question, Why hadn't he done it sooner? They had had a long day, sex wouldn't have been expected. He could have whispered softer. Could have paraphrased what they discussed. Maybe even delayed Tessa's report of what she'd found in the computer. Under the circumstances, a delay would have been reasonable. Logical.

And Riley didn't have an answer for why he hadn't chosen logic over the cheap thrill of holding Tessa. But there was a problem with that particular cheap thrill. It wasn't cheap. And it felt a lot more than just a thrill.

Man, he was *so* in trouble.

There was a knock, just one, and before Riley could even move to sit up in bed, he heard someone insert a key card into the lock. The door opened. He reached out and stopped a very groggy Tessa from overreacting and reaching for a gun that wasn't there anyway.

Their visitor was Beatrice, and she was balancing a tray, some clothes and what appeared to be a laptop computer.

"Dr. Fletcher had to drive to his residence this morning to pick up a few things," the woman explained.

Riley latched right onto that. If Beatrice was telling the truth, it meant Fletcher lived nearby. Or at least seminearby. It could be important info if Tessa and he needed to look elsewhere for the evidence.

Beatrice deposited the items on the table next to the bed. "He'll be back soon. He said I was to bring you a computer so you could check your e-mail."

"Thank you," Riley responded, knowing they wouldn't use it. It was different from the one last night and Fletcher or one of his henchmen had no doubt scrubbed this one clean. Added to that, Fletcher would probably examine any outgoing mail to make sure it didn't breach his security.

"So what's on the agenda today?" Tessa asked Beatrice. She rubbed her hands over her face and yawned.

"More of Phase One."

Riley snagged one of the cups of coffee from the tray and inhaled, hoping the scent alone would wake him up. He wouldn't be drinking any of it. Too big of a risk because Fletcher could have drugged it with a sedative.

Or worse.

"When will we be leaving for the second facility?" he asked Beatrice.

She started for the door, giving her explanation over her shoulder. "Dr. Fletcher has decided that the remaining procedures will be done here at this clinic."

Riley wouldn't know if that was bad news or not until Tessa and he had another look at the computer in Fletcher's office. His gut instinct told him that there was vital information in those files if they got a second crack at them. If they didn't, then somehow they'd have to find the location of that second facility or even Fletcher's residence.

Because Riley wasn't giving up.

The moment Beatrice shut the door behind her, Riley and Tessa got out of bed. Both reached for their clothes and began to dress. Not the clothes that Beatrice had provided, but the jeans and sweater they'd worn the day before. Riley had already inspected them as much as he possibly could for tracing and listening devices.

They kept their movements unhurried in case

they were still being monitored. But with Fletcher supposedly away from the clinic, it was time to proceed with the mission. With good luck, they could be out of here in the next hour or so. With bad luck…

Well, Riley didn't even want to go there.

They had to succeed. Because as much as he hated to admit it, this might be their last and only shot at collaring Colette's killer.

TESSA PEEKED out into the hall, to make sure Beatrice was indeed gone. She was. Thank goodness. No guards in sight, either, which meant they could finally do something about those computer files.

"All clear," she relayed to Riley.

He pressed the button on his watch to engage the signal that would jam and temporarily disrupt Fletcher's surveillance equipment. Tessa prayed that it worked as well as it was supposed to work because by her estimation, they'd need at least ten minutes.

Riley and she made their way down the hall, only to find the door to Fletcher's office locked. Riley extracted a small pin from his watchband and had it open within seconds.

An alarm went off, causing them both to curse. The sound wasn't loud and blaring. More of a warning hum. Unfortunately it wasn't confined to just the room. It seemed to resonate through the entire building. Probably a backup security precaution to alert Fletcher that someone had entered his office.

It was an unanticipated problem. A bad one. Because the jamming device should have neutralized the security system. But Tessa wouldn't let the contingency stop her. She'd already passed the point of no return. If she didn't access the files, now, she might not get another chance.

She ignored the stabbing sound of the alarm and booted up the computer while Riley searched through the desk. Tessa did her own searching, for the hidden files she'd located the night before.

Nothing.

God, they weren't here.

"What's wrong?" Riley asked after he glanced at her.

"The files are gone."

He groaned and motioned for her to continue to look. Tessa did. She resumed her search through the files. Frantically now. Hunting for anything that might be suspicious. But it soon became apparent that she wouldn't find it.

Fletcher had no doubt seen to that.

Riley pressed the communication function on his watch. He held the watch between them so that she'd be able to hear the exchange even over the alarms. "Are you able to get a tracking signal on us?" Riley asked.

"Affirmative," was the response. She recognized

the voice as her father's. "We should have your location pinpointed within the next few minutes. What's your mission status?"

"We struck out," Riley relayed. Not easily. It seemed as if the words caught in his throat. And probably did. Because they'd failed. "Fletcher apparently removed files that Tessa had located last night."

"Do you have anything else?"

Riley glanced at her, then dodged the question. "We'll keep looking."

"Too risky," her father immediately answered. "You've engaged the disruption signal and your cover is in jeopardy. Terminate the mission and inform Dr. Fletcher that you've changed your mind about the procedure. If necessary, use evasive measures to vacate the facility."

"No!" Riley didn't raise his voice beyond a whisper, but it was an angry whisper that conveyed all the frustration and disappointment that Tessa was feeling. "We're too close to stop now."

"That wasn't a request, Agent McDade. It was an order. This mission is terminated. When you've reached a safe rendezvous point, we'll arrange to have you picked up."

The alarms stopped. It happened so quickly, so abruptly, that it plunged the room in total silence. Riley and Tessa didn't hesitate even for a second, because someone had no doubt manually disengaged the alarms. Fletcher probably. The first place he'd look for them was his office. And if he found them, there would be trouble. There was no way they could justify why they were in this room.

Riley caught her arm and got them moving toward the door. He peered out first before they stepped into the hall. They'd only made it a few steps when the first guard rounded the corner.

A second was following closely behind.

"Is there a fire?" Riley shouted. "Is that why the alarms went off?"

He'd asked, hoping to maintain what shred of cover they had left. But it wasn't one of those two guards who answered, but another one, a woman, wearing the same dark blue uniform as her comrades. She came rushing down the hall, as well. Straight toward them.

"What are you doing here?" she demanded.

Riley let go of Tessa's arm so they could move into a better position to respond to the guards. In this case, a better position would mean hand-to-hand combat. That wasn't Tessa's first choice of self-defense since they were outnumbered and unarmed.

"The alarms frightened my wife," Riley lied.

If the guard believed that even a little, she didn't show it. Her eyes darkened. "You were in Dr. Fletcher's office again."

And it wasn't a question.

"We were looking for a way out," Tessa volunteered. "Because we thought the place was on fire."

"Come on, darling," Riley said to her. "I've had enough of this. We're leaving now."

The guard stepped to the side, blocking their path. "That won't be possible," she said.

And with that she drew her weapon and aimed it right at them.

RILEY KNEW their situation had just seriously escalated. John Abbot's order to *use evasive measures to vacate the facility* was now a reality.

The female guard stepped toward them. She kept a firm grip on her lethal-looking semiautomatic. The others drew their weapons, as well, and walked in Tessa's and his direction.

This could play one of two ways. He could continue to protest Tessa's and his innocence, or they could brace themselves to fight their way out.

Riley figured no matter what he did, it would come down to a fight.

"Drop back," he mumbled to Tessa when the guard took one step too many.

Tessa lunged back into the office, creating a timely visual distraction, just as Riley reached out and latched onto the female guard's gun. She didn't give it up without a fight, though.

And that's where Tessa came in.

Diving to the floor, she reached out and snagged the guard's leg. One hard yank and the woman was off balanced. Riley used that to snatch the gun from her hand.

He didn't stop there.

Praying that Tessa would take cover, he shoved the woman out of the way and positioned himself to aim at the other guards.

He was about a second too late.

One of Fletcher's other henchmen fired and Riley dropped down so he wouldn't be shot. The female guard wasn't so lucky. She took the full impact in the chest. Before she'd even hit the floor, Riley took out the guard with two shots to the head.

The other guard turned and sprinted out of the hall. Escaping.

"Hell," Riley snarled. They couldn't let him get away and alert God knew how many others. Beatrice was likely lurking around, and by now Fletcher could have returned from his errands.

Tessa obviously understood that because she hurried out of the office and they raced down the hall after the escapee. She stopped only long enough to grab the handgun from the now dead guard.

"I'll go in low," she informed him as they approached the point where the hall intersected another. It was a danger zone where anything or anybody could be lying in wait. Too many blind spots. Too many shadows.

Tessa stooped down so she could approach the zone from the low level. Riley took the high point. He made a split-second glance around the corner and was only mildly relieved that he didn't come face-to-face with a guard or anyone else connected with Fletcher.

"Clear," Riley advised her, and they started down that particular section of the clinic.

They worked silently, in unison. Giving a little more than a cursory inspection to each room they passed. Even with the impending danger, Riley noticed that Tessa was good at teamwork. Something he sincerely appreciated. Unfortunately it wasn't always possible to know if the mix was right until something went wrong.

And things had definitely gone wrong.

The last door at the end of the hall was closed. And locked. If the guard was waiting inside, he'd likely anticipate them and use the opportunity of their forcing the door to fire. Still, they'd have to risk it.

"Cover me," Riley said.

He rammed his shoulder into the door, but a hefty shove didn't cause it to budge. Using the heel of his boot, Riley gave it a good hard kick, splintering it apart. He thanked his lucky stars for shoddy workmanship, and they cautiously went inside.

It was unmanned.

For now.

But that probably wasn't routine since it appeared to be Fletcher's command post. A center for communications and security equipment, and judging from the monitors fixed to the wall, it was also used for surveillance.

He located the missing guard.

Since the monitors were labeled and motion-activated, Riley knew the man was in the clinic entrance—only one room away. He was probably waiting to ambush them. But that wasn't Riley's primary worry. He wondered if the guard had let his boss know what was going on.

"Can you cut communications?" he asked Tessa while he kept a close watch on the door. After all, they had no idea how many guards were on the premises. If they could stop the information flow, that might keep Fletcher out of it for a while.

Tessa worked her way across the room. Searching. Until she reached the keyboard.

"Done," she said after less than a minute. "We need to find the surveillance videos. If we can retrieve them and apprehend that guard, we might be able to bluff our way out of this and Fletcher might not figure out why we were here."

True. It might give them a very slim shot at continuing the investigation. Plus, there was the added bonus that there might be something on those tapes that would incriminate Fletcher. Judging from the type of equipment in the command post, there were probably at least a hundred hours of surveillance on one single tape. Since they were motion-activated, those one hundred hours could cover days if not weeks of activity.

While he guarded the door, Tessa scoured through the equipment tucked into the far corner of the room and located the surveillance feed. She pulled out a tape, shoved it into the back waist of her jeans and tossed a second tape to Riley. He snatched it from the air and did the same.

"Oh, Judas!" he heard her say.

Riley glanced in her direction to see what had prompted her response and soon saw the numbers on the tiny black rectangular box just beneath the surveillance equipment. Not stationary numbers, either.

They were scrolling down.

Fast.

"It's a timer," Tessa said, already moving away from it. "And it's set to go off in three minutes."

Riley cursed. Three minutes. Probably an explosive device that would bring down the whole place. They could take the time to disarm it, but it was a huge risk.

"Let's go," Riley ordered.

They wasted no time making their way out of the command post and, still hoping they'd have the element of surprise, they rushed into the entrance.

No guard.

He'd either moved to another room or had left the building. Not a comforting thought. Especially since they would have to rush outside with a gunman possibly waiting for them. But they didn't have time to go back through the building to find an alternate escape route.

Tessa stooped low again when they approached the reinforced door that led to the front of the clinic. It was where the limo had dropped them off the night before. The limo was gone, but there were now three cars outside. Cars without passengers or drivers.

That meant nothing, of course.

Since they couldn't wait any longer, Riley led them out the door, and Tessa adjusted her position so they were back-to-back. Using the building for cover, they hurried to the edge of the small parking area but soon realized they were out in the middle of nowhere. There were no other buildings, no other signs of life, just a thick wooded area that practically circled, and canopied, the clinic.

Since it was close, and since time wasn't on their side, Riley headed for the west portion of the property. They didn't get far.

A shot rang out.

It was a loud crash of sound that tore through the air, and Riley could have sworn it missed his head by a fraction of an inch. Not a result of an explosion, either.

But a bullet.

He instinctively pushed Tessa to the ground, but she obviously had some strong instincts of her own. She rolled to her stomach and levered herself so that she was ready to return fire.

Riley dropped to the ground, as well.

And he waited.

He didn't have to wait long.

The guard ducked out from the other side of the building. He had his weapon aimed and ready to kill. But then, so did Riley.

And so did Tessa.

They both fired at the man and both their shots found the intended target. The man tumbled into a heap on the ground.

"Let's get out of here," Riley insisted. He caught Tessa's arm, yanked her to her feet, and they sprinted toward the cover of the thick woods.

Just as the building exploded into a ball of fire.

Chapter Eight

With Tessa running hard right behind him, Riley cut through a narrow section of oak trees and came to a stop at the edge of a pasture-lined country road. It was a good two miles from the clinic. A safe enough distance.

He hoped.

If not, then at least the weapons they'd taken meant they were armed for a second round.

He saw Tessa press the homing device on her watch. Without Fletcher's security measures, the device would lead the SIU recovery team to Tessa and him.

It wouldn't take long, either.

Riley estimated a half hour max. But even if the homing device failed, that mammoth explosion would have certainly garnered SIU's attention. It'd certainly garnered his. Another minute in that clinic and they would have been dead.

Oh, man.

They were lucky they'd even seen that denotation device in time. If Fletcher had hidden it, *really* hidden it, then the man might have succeeded in claiming two more victims.

"I'm sorry," Tessa said, gulping in some hard breaths. She sank to the ground and rested the back of her head against a tree. What she didn't do was put down her weapon. She kept it ready in her hands. "I didn't notice the detonation mechanism when I pulled out those tapes."

"No reason to apologize. I didn't see it, either." But he damn sure should have. He'd known from the onset that Fletcher didn't play fair, and that device was exactly the kind of surprise he should have anticipated the doctor would use.

Riley dropped down onto the ground and swept a vigilant glance around the woods, just in case one of Fletcher's guards had managed to follow them. Not likely, but he'd obviously been wrong about Fletcher before.

"Are you okay?" he asked her.

Tessa nodded. "You?"

He glanced down at their clothes to make sure neither had been injured in the gunfight. Tessa looked sweaty and tired, and there were smears of dirt on her face, but other than that, she seemed unharmed.

Thank God.

"I'm all in one piece."

He hesitated, trying to figure out how he should say what he needed to say to her. After mentally testing a few scenarios, he finally decided he couldn't make it sound palatable. Best to go for the direct approach. "I want to keep looking. I want to keep digging until we have the proof to nail Fletcher."

With her breath still gusting from the long run, Tessa shook her head and raked her damp hair away from her face. "You heard what the director said. This mission's been terminated."

It was the exact response he'd expected from her.

So why did it rile him?

Maybe because he thought things had changed between them. That they'd developed a sort of… fondness for each other. An empathy.

But who the heck was he kidding?

The only thing that had developed between them was a good old-fashioned case of lust.

Wasn't it?

Man, he hoped that's all there was to it. Because the alternative would complicate things at a time when he needed no more complications.

"For once, can't you just go with your instincts?" He tossed the question at her. "Because we're close to getting him, Tessa. I can feel it."

She opened her mouth to answer but didn't get the chance. Her watch made a soft beep. The tiny sound was an indication that someone at SIU had latched onto their tracking signal and was trying to contact them. Probably to see if they were alive. Tessa reached to answer it, but Riley put his hand over hers, stopping her.

"We could tell them we're in pursuit," he suggested. Except it was a little more than a suggestion. It was more like an ultimatum. "That wouldn't be a lie. Fletcher is probably somewhere in the area, and if we get a vehicle, some equipment and start searching now, we'd find him."

Tessa's gaze stayed firmly on him and Riley watched the intense debate going on in those baby blues. What he didn't see was surrender or any other indication that she would go along with this.

Just as he'd expected.

"I'm sorry," Tessa finally said. She moved his hand away so she could press the button on her watch. "Agent Abbot here."

"What's your situation?" Riley heard Tessa's father ask.

She glanced at him first. Just a glance. But she didn't wait for him to respond. "Agent McDade and I are safe, but the facility was destroyed."

"Yes. We saw the explosion, and I have an Evidence Response Team on the way there now to lock down the area and sift for evidence."

"We also had to return fire during our escape. Some of Fletcher's employees were killed."

"You know the regs," Abbot commented. "Don't discuss the incident until you've both given your statements and been debriefed."

In other words, Tessa and he would be kept apart for at least forty-eight hours. Normally that wouldn't have bothered Riley, but this time it did. Mainly because they had a lot of unfinished business. And it wasn't all personal, either. He hadn't given up on convincing her to go after Fletcher.

"What about your suspect?" Abbot asked.

Tessa looked at him again, and Riley gave her a go-ahead nod. "He wasn't in the clinic at the time of the explosion. At least, that's what one of his employees told us. We did manage to retrieve surveillance tapes but nothing else." She cleared her throat. "We're considering whether to pursue the suspect since he's probably in the vicinity."

"There'll be no pursuit," Abbot ordered without hesitation. "I have a helicopter en route to pick you up. After you've debriefed and gotten some crew rest, you need to report to the Alpha team mission director in Denver so you can close out the classified reports on your last ops."

Not exactly busywork, Riley knew, but it probably wasn't mission-critical, either. It'd mean that Tessa would be stuck in a security vault for days doing paperwork. In Denver, no less. She sure wouldn't be out trying to track down Fletcher here in Texas.

And she wouldn't be with him.

"Agent McDade," Abbot continued. "Estimated time of arrival for your transport vehicle is twelve minutes. Since this was a back-to-back ops for you, you're to make your reports and then begin mandatory leave. I'm recommending a minimum of a week in which time you'll do nothing that involves this or any other mission. Understood?"

Oh, yeah. Riley understood. Abbot was ordering him to back off. Way off. And during that time, Fletcher would almost certainly get away.

"Copy," Riley answered.

It wasn't an agreement to comply. And Tessa knew it. Riley saw a muscle jump in her cheek. Thankfully she didn't voice what had caused that disapproving facial reaction until she'd disengaged communication with her father.

"This could cost you your career," she pointed out. "You know that."

"I know. And that should tell you just how important this is to me."

"Believe me, I know how important this is, Riley, but turning renegade isn't the way to do it. Return to headquarters and regroup."

"If I do that, Fletcher will go so far underground we'll never find him."

In the distance, he heard the sound of an approaching helicopter. Tessa's transport.

Time was already running out fast.

"I don't want you to do this," she said. Not a gruffly barked order like the one her father had issued to him moments earlier. But a request. One with an unspoken plea laced through it.

It was exactly what Riley needed. That plea reminded him of what was truly at stake here. Fletcher had already killed at least one agent, and he would kill Tessa if he got the chance. And that was the best argument Riley could make for leaving her out of this.

Yes.

Even though he hadn't immediately recognized it as such, her refusal was a gift. Now he wouldn't have to worry about her safety. He wouldn't have to watch his every step and pray that he could keep her safe. For once, her penchant for following the rules would make his life a lot easier.

"I don't want you to change your mind," Riley insisted. "Go to Denver. Do your reports."

Her eyes widened slightly. Then narrowed not so slightly. Probably because she was confused by his sudden change of heart. "Is this some kind of reverse psychology?"

He shook his head. "Absolutely not. I don't want you anywhere near Fletcher when I go after him. That's the way this should have gone down all along. Just him and me. That way, you'll be safe."

Another muscle twitch in her jaw. "And if *being safe* isn't what I want?"

That touched him in a way that nothing else could have because he knew how much it cost her just to consider helping him. "It's what you want," he decided for her. "Going to Denver is the only choice I'm giving you."

She stared at him. Riley stared back, trying to make her understand that this was nonnegotiable. And in those moments, a thousand things passed between them. Not just mission-related things, either. Things that were better left alone and unsaid.

Too bad he didn't do just that.

"I didn't want this to happen between us," he insisted.

That was true. No shades of gray or doubt. Riley didn't want his feelings for her to deepen. And it shouldn't have been an issue because there were so many logical reasons to keep their relationship strictly business.

But then, there were all the illogical reasons.

Feelings. Emotions.

Attraction that just wouldn't go away.

The air changed between them. Or something changed, that was for sure. For lack of a better word, there was an energy. It seemed to pinpoint all his focus solely on her. On her eyes. On her mouth. And Riley knew there was only one place for this to go.

Cursing his lack of willpower and the insane thing he was about to do, Riley reached out, curved his hand around the back of her neck and hauled her to him. She landed against his chest. She didn't resist, something she probably should have done, and Riley finally saw the surrender in her eyes.

Not good.

It was a really bad time for her to do anything involving surrender. Yet, it was the only thing he'd wanted to see in the depths of all that blue.

Tessa made the next move. Her mouth came to his. Man, did it. Her moist, sweet, hot mouth. The kiss was hard and hungry, and in that moment, Riley knew if there was any battle against her left to be fought, he'd lose it.

Hell, he *wanted* to lose.

The kiss was a rough, swift assault. Her fingers dug into his shoulders, fighting to bring him even closer. Not possible since they were already plastered against each other.

Riley did some fighting of his own. He battled with her, jockeying for position, as if this kiss were a life-and-death matter. As if this kiss could fix everything that had gone wrong. As if it could redeem him.

And maybe it could.

Maybe it was the proof that he'd been looking for. The affirmation that he hadn't died that day with Colette.

The sound of the helicopter got louder. Much louder. And Tessa pulled away from him. Not completely, though. She kept her arms around him as the helicopter eased down in the pasture. The pilot frantically motioned for her to board.

Hesitating, Riley felt her fingers brush over the surveillance tape that he'd crammed into the back waist of his jeans. Tessa pulled away ever farther and looked at him. He expected her to demand that he give that tape to her so she could turn it in to headquarters.

But she didn't.

"Promise me if you're around flying bullets, you'll duck," Tessa whispered. "Don't follow in your father's footsteps. No Purple Hearts."

"I promise," he lied.

Worse, they both knew it was a lie.

She let her gaze linger on him for several too short moments before she pushed herself away, got up and walked toward the helicopter.

Riley got up, as well. Not to follow her. He wouldn't do that, even though every part of him except his brain wanted him to do just that.

Fortunately his brain would win this one.

He wouldn't let his heart make a decision that would endanger Tessa.

Riley watched as she stepped aboard the chopper. She didn't even glance back. Which was a good thing. He didn't want to have to remember the look that he knew would be in her eyes.

Not regret. But disappointment.

The pilot immediately lifted off, the helicopter blades whipping up the wind and sending a circular spray of slivered leaves and dirt flying through the air. And Riley just kept on watching.

Until the chopper was out of sight.

Then Riley turned and headed back into the thick woods. In the opposite direction from his own transport.

Away from Tessa.

Away from the life and the career he'd made for himself.

One way or another, and no matter what the cost, he would bring Fletcher down.

Chapter Nine

Dr. Barton Fletcher stared at the black-and-white photograph for several minutes, until he felt the dangerous anger bubbling up inside him.

And he didn't even try to contain that anger.

He grabbed the photo from his desk, ripped it to shreds and threw the debris into the fireplace. The crystal decanter followed. Crashing. Slivering into a thousand shimmering pieces. The expensive bourbon inside sent the flames lashing in the hearth.

"Damn them."

The two of them had tried to ruin him. Of course, he had to take some of the blame for this. He should have trusted his instincts, and his instincts had told him that they were not who they had claimed to be, that they were not to be trusted.

His instincts had been right.

Now the clinic was gone. Reduced to rubble and ash. It was a rental, so the building itself was no huge loss, but the equipment inside would be expensive to replace. As would the three employees who'd died. It didn't matter that he didn't even know their names or had even a vague recollection of their faces.

They were his.

His.

And that's why retribution for their deaths had to be hard and swift.

It had taken him almost three weeks of digging, but finally he had what he needed. He picked up the phone as the orangy flames devoured what was left of the photograph.

"Agents Tessa Abbot and Riley McDade," Fletcher said to the person who answered the phone. "Find them. *Now.* I want them both."

ADJUSTING HER equipment bag, her Chinese takeout and the half dozen or so yellowing sales flyers that she'd gathered up from her covered entrance, Tessa unlocked the door to her D.C. condo. The security system immediately began to whine and she reached inside to press the buttons on the keypad to disarm it. Glancing down on the foyer floor, she noticed that she'd killed another ficus plant.

"Welcome home," she mumbled.

And that was *home* in a generic sense.

She'd lived in this particular condo almost a year and hadn't gotten around to furnishing the place.

Well, except for her repeated attempts to have a Feng Shui thing with ficus plants. But other than dead flora still in their pots, it was definitely a bare-bones room—a sofa and an entertainment center that she hadn't completely figured out how to operate.

Tessa tossed her equipment bag and the sales flyers next to the ficus and glanced in the direction of the phone still perched on the arm of the sofa. Right where she'd left it almost three weeks ago before leaving with Riley for the Fletcher assignment. Because the room was dark, she had no trouble seeing the pulsing red message light. Her heart jumped at the possibility that Riley might have called while she was in Denver.

And Tessa cursed her juvenile, hormone-induced reaction.

There was no reason for Riley to stay in touch. None. It wasn't as if their relationship had been personal.

Except for her.

A thought that riled and annoyed her.

Still, that didn't stop her from crossing the room— hurriedly crossing, at that—and nearly tripping over her own feet. She pressed the button on the phone to listen to her messages.

The first one was from her father, asking her if she'd heard from Riley. The second was from Karen Sandoval, a friend and fellow SIU agent, who wanted Tessa to call her at home.

Probably to ask if she'd heard from Riley.

Heaven knew, enough people had quizzed her about that while she was in Denver. She hadn't lied, exactly. But then she hadn't told the truth, either. She hadn't informed anyone that Riley had almost certainly continued the mission that he'd been ordered to terminate.

Hissing out a weary breath, she decided that Karen, her father and their questions about Riley would have to wait. "A long bubble bath and a glass of wine get priority tonight," Tessa mumbled.

Every part of her body seemed achy and sore, and Tessa gave her shoulder a test rotation to see if it would help to loosen up her muscles. It didn't. Desk duty for the past two weeks had taken more of a toll than an intense field ops.

She could blame that in part on the nonstop, tormenting images of Riley McDade. Specifically, images of his seminaked body and that kiss. Not the fake ones they'd shared during the ops. *The* kiss. The real one in the forest before the helicopter had arrived. The kiss she'd relived a thousand times.

The feel of his mouth on hers.

The way he fit against her body.

The taste of him.

Especially his taste.

Damn him.

How the heck had she let him get to her like this?

Nothing could come of it, of course. With her possible promotion on the horizon, she could soon be a rookie mission commander. A desk job, yes, but it was something that she'd strived for since she'd become an agent. A position that required a spotless record. A position she respected.

As did her father.

Besides, Riley was now a renegade. He hadn't contacted anyone in the agency. Not that she'd officially heard that. But if he'd checked in, then people wouldn't have been questioning her to find out where he was.

Well, wherever he was, he was obviously headed in a different direction from her personal career path, and it was possible she'd never see him again. Tessa was a little surprised to realize that the possibility of that caused her heart to ache.

Yes, Riley was arrogant, pigheaded and a badass rebel. But it would take a lifetime for her to forget that he was also the most memorable man she'd ever met.

Forcing that truly depressing thought aside, Tessa peeled off her jacket, turned on the too dim living room light and then the radio—the one part of the entertainment center she did know how to operate. The restless, pulsing sounds of a popular hip hop song poured through the room. She immediately changed the station because she was restless enough without the music adding more.

"It's me," she heard someone say.

The voice jolted through her and before it even registered in her brain, she turned to dive toward her equipment bag to get her weapon. But then, she realized it wasn't just *someone.*

It was Riley.

He'd been so much on her mind, that for a moment Tessa thought he was a mirage.

He wasn't.

Definitely the real thing.

Dressed all in black and looking as if he'd just stepped away from a covert ops, he was here. Right here. Standing in the doorway of her bedroom.

He had his hands bracketed on each side of the doorjamb. His gunmetal gaze fastened firmly on her. He looked like the answer to every woman's hot fantasy.

Well, her fantasies anyway.

"How did you get in?" she asked.

Not exactly the greeting she'd rehearsed if she ever saw him again, but the question had just leaped out of her mouth. It was certainly better than saying something about how relieved she was to see him.

His stupid renegade antics hadn't gotten him killed.

"I came in through the French doors off your bedroom," he explained. Calmly. As if breaking and entering was as common as brushing his teeth. For him, maybe it was. "I temporarily disarmed your security system."

Oh. "It's supposed to be tamper-proof."

He shrugged. "Nothing's tamper-proof."

Touché. And that was true on a lot of levels, especially personal ones.

He cocked his head to the side. "Are you planning to call your father and turn me in?"

It was a good question. Very good.

Too bad Tessa didn't have a very good answer.

She countered with a question of her own. "Why did you come here?"

He gave her a considering stare, shook his head as if suddenly aggravated, and pushed himself away from the door. He walked closer. Slow, easy, calculated steps. Tiger steps. As if he were stalking a prey.

Or a mate.

That last part was probably just her insane imagination.

Or much to her disgust, wishful thinking.

"I thought you might be interested in what happened after we parted ways." His words were slow and easy, a verbal stroll with his accent kissing the words.

Tessa nodded and swallowed hard when he stopped just inches in front of her. So close that she caught his scent. His well-worn black leather jacket. His deodorant soap. And the unique smell of the equally unique man.

"I reviewed the surveillance tape we got from the clinic." Riley took the tape in question from the pocket inside his jacket and tossed it onto her sofa. "By the way, thanks for giving me the opportunity to check it out."

"You're welcome." Since his tone had turned businesslike, Tessa added some aloofness to her own. "The techs didn't find anything useful on the tape I had. Well, except for the fact that Fletcher was running a scam with the DNA manipulation, but we already knew that."

Another step closer. Too close. A definite violation of personal space. "Yes." He let that hum between them for several seconds. "Does the name 'Brice Marden' mean anything to you?"

Tessa had anticipated several things he might say, but she hadn't expected their discussion to move in that direction. "You mean, the artist?"

"Yeah, that's the one." Riley glanced around the bare walls of the condo and frowned. "Why don't you have any art in this place?"

Okay. So, she hadn't expected that, either. "Is that conversation, or is this about what you found on the tape?"

"Both."

She shook her head. "I don't understand. What does one have to do with the other?"

"Just an observation. I figured you must like art if you can recognize a genuine Picasso from a fake in Fletcher's office, and if you recognized an artist who's not a household name. Well, not in my household anyway."

Riley turned, angling his body so that he was still close but not facing her, and he leaned his back against the snack bar that separated the kitchen from the living room. "On the surveillance tape, Fletcher mentioned that he'd just bought an untitled Brice Marden."

"And?" Tessa tried to sound nonchalant but failed miserably when she realized where all of this was leading. "You found the paper trail for the sale?"

He nodded. "The seller hasn't met Fletcher—yet. It was an e-transaction. But Fletcher's due to pick up the painting tomorrow evening at a gallery in Houston."

"He won't show. He'll send one of his employees," she quickly pointed out.

"No doubt. But employees can be followed just as well as Fletcher can be. He's gone underground, Tessa. He's trying to stay out of sight while the heat dies down, but that painting will lead me right to him."

The agent part of her wanted to celebrate his success. Riley had done it. He'd closed in on a killer. But there was another part of her that was suddenly terrified for him. After all, he had no backup. No support from headquarters. He was a lone renegade walking into a lion's den.

"I can talk to my father," she offered. "Perhaps get you some assistance from the local authorities—"

"No. I don't want you involved in this." He mumbled something under his breath. "That's not why I'm here. You were right to leave on the helicopter that day."

This time there was no businesslike tone in Riley's voice, but Tessa wasn't sure what emotion had replaced it. Something, though. Something that scared her far more than facing down a killer.

"What do you mean?" she asked.

"Fletcher was on to us," Riley admitted. "I heard him say it on the surveillance tape. He chose his words carefully, but he indicated to Beatrice that his suspicions were why he wouldn't take us to that second facility." His gaze came back to her. "He's looking for us, Tessa."

Along with a lot of other scenarios, she'd considered that. However, considering it was totally different from having it confirmed. She swallowed hard. "Probably. But he won't find us. He won't be able to get through the layers of SIU security."

Riley reached out, touched her arm with his fingers and rubbed softly. A comforting gesture. Probably not meant to arouse her.

Even though she fought it, the sensations rippled through.

"Fletcher might," he said. "That's why I'm here. To warn you. I figured you were safe while you were shut away in a vault in Denver. But here, you need to be careful."

Tessa had to push the effects of that rippling sensation aside so she could respond to what he was saying. "I'm always careful, Riley."

However, for the first time in her career, maybe her entire life, Tessa wondered if that was true. She hadn't been careful in guarding her heart.

And she was paying for it.

Because now that he'd delivered his message, in a few minutes Riley would no doubt leave, and even if he collared Fletcher, she might never see him again.

"Why the look?" he asked.

Tessa wanted to deny there was a look, but instead she just tried to change her expression.

Judging from Riley's frown, she didn't succeed. Not even a little.

He hooked his fingers into the waist of her jeans and pulled her closer. "Why do you do that?"

"Do what?" And that would have been a much more effective comeback if Tessa hadn't had to repeat it just to give it some sound.

The corner of his mouth lifted a fraction. A simple gesture that was anything but simple coming from Riley. "Close down. Pretend none of this matters."

"Because it's easier."

Which was a lie.

Nothing about this was *easier.*

"We're not partners anymore," he informed her. He tugged her another inch closer. Then another.

Until his thigh was right against hers. And until the heat was blazing through her like wildfire.

Tessa tried one last time. "But we're both still SIU agents."

"Well, one of us is anyway. My future at the agency is in question."

And with that he leaned in and brushed his mouth over hers.

"Riley—"

But saying his name was as far as Tessa got. Because there was no argument in the world she could voice that would stop her from wanting him. Even the time they'd spent apart—time that she'd hoped would help cleanse her mind of him—had only made her want him more.

"I don't understand this," she whispered, with his mouth hovering right over hers.

"Neither do I."

And after admitting that, he went in for the capture. He took her mouth. Claiming it. It was pure finesse. Raw emotion. All laced with need, want, desire. All the emotions they'd tried to keep at bay while they'd pretended to be lovers.

Nothing about this was a pretense.

Nothing.

Tessa tried to catch her breath. But couldn't. And decided she didn't want her breath anyway. What she wanted was *this*. She wanted Riley. She wanted his mouth on her. She wanted to feel all the things that he could make her feel. All the things he was offering.

He moved slowly and yet it seemed as if everything else happened fast. So fast. The pulse drumming in her head. Her breath. The fire that raced through her. It was as if she were caught in a whirlwind of emotion and sensations.

His mouth didn't stop, either. He continued to kiss her. First, just her lips. Then he worked his way down. To her chin. And lower. Until he finally reached that place on her neck that she'd put off-limits at the clinic. But Riley obviously no longer considered it forbidden territory. His mouth lingered there.

Touching.

Teasing.

Arousing.

Until Tessa had to have more. She circled her arms around him and jerked him toward her, until they were plastered against each other. Body against body. Her breasts against his chest. Every part of him against every part of her.

Riley moved slightly away from her, turned and pinned her against the wall. Not that she was planning to go anywhere. But he gathered her wrists in his left hand and lifted them over her head, pressing them against the cool painted surface. He slid his other hand over the front of her loose cable-knit sweater.

Tessa heard herself moan. A deep sound of need. And was surprised by just how much need there was swelling up inside her.

He eased his hand lower. Beneath her sweater. His fingers slid over her stomach, over her bare skin, creating a pulsing ache that was already starting to demand relief. But he didn't go in the direction of that ache. Instead he worked his way up.

To her breasts.

There, he sparked a different kind of ache. One so strong that Tessa gasped for air.

Riley pushed down the cups of her bra and, without breaking eye contact with her, wet his fingertips with his tongue and then slid those now moist fingers over her nipples.

Tessa got so caught up in the pleasure, the sensations, that she almost forgot that she shouldn't be only on the receiving end of this. There were things she wanted to do to him. Things she'd fantasized about all week. Now, she would get to live out that fantasy.

She lifted her right leg, slowly. No random movement, either. She slid her leg between his and used her thigh to apply some light pressure to his erection.

Her pulse jumped when she heard Riley's suddenly ragged breath. And then he cursed. Not mild profanity, either. A collection of words that should have made her blush, but instead kicked the fire inside her up a notch.

"If we're going to finish this," she managed to say, "we should go to the bedroom."

Riley shook his head, and for a moment she was afraid he might have come to his senses.

Thank goodness, he hadn't.

"We're not the missionary type," he told her, repeating what they'd said in the clinic. His voice was slightly rough. Like the still-damp thumb he swiped over her right nipple. A movement that caused her to see double. "Or the bed type. Besides, I want to take the edge off for you. No regrets, Tessa. Not about this."

Not understanding, she fought her way through the haze so she could speak. "What do you mean?"

Riley didn't answer. Instead he showed her.

Mercy, did he ever.

Still pinning her in place, not with his hand but his solid, lean body, he unzipped her jeans and he slipped his hand inside. She felt his fingers, warm and rough, rub across her stomach. And lower, past the top of her panties. And lower still. Until his fingers found her. Wet and hot. He made his way through the slick moisture.

One touch, and her breath shuddered.

One touch, and he already had her close to release.

Riley made a sound, too. Part moan, as if the sensations were torture. Tessa knew how he felt. It was sweet, relentless torture for her, as well. Because he kept moving.

His fingers, sliding hot inside her now.

His mouth, sucking not so gently on that delicate place on her neck. Until it was almost unbearable.

Yet he continued.

Those gifted strokes of his fingers took her almost to the brink. Almost. And then he pulled her back so he could give her even more.

Tessa, uncertain of just how much more she could take, reached out and pressed her hand against that hard ridge in the front of his jeans. But he didn't let her do that for long.

Riley snagged her wrists again. "You'll be able to think this through if your body isn't burning."

Ah, now she got it. If she were semisated, she might change her mind about having sex with him.

She wouldn't change her mind, of course.

She would have never allowed that first kiss if she'd planned to stop.

So, Tessa slung off his grip, caught his shoulders and reversed their positions. And she wasn't gentle with him, either. They were past that point. His back landed, hard, against the wall. A little maneuver that earned her a husky laugh and a few raunchy suggestions.

Still, Riley never missed a beat. Or rather, he never missed a stroke with those clever fingers. In fact, he turned up the heat.

The room didn't just turn, it whirled. Her breath vanished. Her heart slammed against her chest. And she was lost. Willingly lost. But Tessa didn't intend to be *lost* without him.

Too bad Riley had other ideas.

"You first," he said, and he obviously meant it.

He hooked his arm around her waist, holding her in place. Stroking her until the fire inside her raged and burned so blistering hot that she couldn't bear it any longer.

Still, as powerful as it was, that alone wouldn't have sent her over the edge. No. Tessa could have still pulled back enough to take Riley with her.

"Tessa," he said, and she was lost.

Her name was a sweet whispered plea that sent the fire blazing out of control, until it consumed her. She could hold on no longer.

Riley's touch released her and set her free.

The spiral of pleasure racked her body. She felt her legs give way, but Riley was right there to catch her. Right there with a tender kiss that made her heart ache for more. Yes, he'd sated her body. For now.

But that only made Tessa want him more.

More was exactly what she planned to give him, too. After she'd gathered her breath.

And if the phone hadn't rung.

The sound shot through the room.

"Let the machine get it," Riley insisted, pulling her back to him. "I'm not finished with you yet."

A comment that sent her heart racing all over again.

"I'm the one with some finishing to do," Tessa informed him. She went after his zipper. No easy task, since his erection was testing the limits of his jeans.

Even though she was giving almost all her attention to ridding Riley of his clothes, she heard the caller when the answering machine kicked in.

"Tessa?" It was Karen Sandoval, the agent who'd left the other message on her machine. "I've been trying to get in touch with you for the past two hours."

With that reminder, Tessa realized she'd turned off her cell phone during the flight and had forgotten to turn it back on. "Mercy," she snarled. She pulled back and looked at Riley. "Hold this thought," she said, sliding her fingers over him.

Cursing Karen and whatever had prompted the phone call, Tessa momentarily untangled herself from Riley, which was no simple maneuver since they were wrapped around each other. She hurried across the room, intending to find out what had gotten her friend so obviously agitated. However, she stopped in her tracks when she heard the next part of the message.

"Your father's on the way to your place." Karen warned her. "Something's come up."

And right on cue, her doorbell rang.

Tessa didn't have to guess who it was, and she didn't have to speculate about what her father's reaction would be to seeing Riley. He would take him to headquarters to *speak* to the chief. He would likely be suspended. Or worse. Of course, that would be the appropriate thing to do. It was what the regs insisted be done.

But she couldn't let that happen.

She just couldn't.

"Wait in my bedroom." Tessa latched onto Riley's arm to do her part to take him there. "I'll get rid of him as fast as I can."

"I won't hide from him."

Great. Just great. Riley intended to argue with her attempts to save his butt. Well, this was no arguing matter as far as Tessa was concerned. "We're going to salvage your career," she informed. "And that won't happen if my father finds you here."

Tessa all but pushed Riley in the direction of her bedroom while she tried to fix her clothes and while Karen continued to talk through the answering machine. "Anyway, it's obvious you're not there, or you'd be picking up. Right, Tessa?"

Karen cursed.

Again, Tessa almost answered the phone, but Riley wasn't moving nearly as fast as she wanted him to move. Her father had a key to her condo, and she didn't want him using it. And he probably would. Since her car was out front, he knew she was here.

"Heck, I might as well just say this so your father doesn't blindside you with it," Karen went on. "We just got back the results from the routine physical you took this morning before you left Denver."

That captured Tessa's complete attention.

But not nearly as much as Karen's next remark.

"Tessa, you're pregnant."

Chapter Ten

Riley held his breath.

And he waited.

Because he didn't know what else to do. There were a lot of thoughts racing around in his head and he didn't know how to deal with any of them.

Tessa snatched up the phone. "It's true?" she asked Karen. She paused. Shook her head. "But it can't be. The test is obviously wrong."

And Riley waited some more. Until he heard Tessa say, "It was positive."

That didn't sound like a question to him.

Oh, man.

When the full impact of that nonquestion registered, it felt as if someone had punched him in the solar plexus with a sledge hammer. Not once, but repeatedly.

The air in his lungs was gone.

Completely gone.

Sucked right out of him.

He stepped back, bracketing his hands on his hips to stop himself from doing something totally dignity-reducing such as falling. But, by God, he needed some kind of support right now. Then again, so did Tessa. Probably more than he did.

"I didn't see this one coming," Riley finally managed to say.

Tessa shook her head. Jerky, almost frantic motions, and she dropped the phone in the direction of its cradle. She missed. "Neither did I."

She made a small, helpless sound that came from deep within her throat. A rattle of breath. Her palms landed flat against the wall.

Riley tried to think of what the heck he should do to make this situation better for both of them. No words of wisdom came to mind, but plenty of thoughts did.

Bad thoughts.

He wasn't exactly father material by anyone's standards. He'd been shot at too many times to count. His body was a patchwork of scars from his previous assignments.

But that particular "bad thought" was just for starters.

"Hell, in the past two years, I haven't even been able to commit to a phone plan," he mumbled.

Why, he didn't know.

Unfortunately he'd mumbled a little louder than he should have.

Tessa lifted her head, met his gaze and laughed. A single burst of sound. Not from humor, either. Pure uncut irony. "Riley, this isn't your problem."

That wasn't what he'd wanted to hear.

"Oh, yeah?" He silently cursed. "This isn't going to turn into a discussion about how I'm not a part of this. If you have objections or doubts about how all of this will play out, then they'll have to keep, all right? I think we'll both need time to deal with this little bombshell."

She nodded. Not exactly a gesture of compliance, though. Nor was it because she agreed with him. Her response was more likely from shock.

A response Riley totally understood.

And that was exactly how John Abbot found them when he unlocked the door and opened it.

Tessa thankfully didn't try to hide him again, probably because she was too stunned to move. But Riley wouldn't have run for cover anyway. Not before he'd heard Karen's news, and definitely not afterward.

Right now, they needed to deal not only with John Abbot's visit but also with the fact that their world had just been turned upside down.

Abbot didn't seem surprised to find him there. His gaze landed on Tessa first. Just a cursory look. Then he aimed a at glance Riley.

Not so cursory.

It was laced with displeasure and probably even some disgust. And then Abbot looked at the phone.

"You heard," her father concluded. He stepped inside and shut the door behind him.

"Karen says it's true," Tessa offered. "Is it?"

Abbot hesitated. Not long. And unlike Tessa, his motions weren't frantic but slow and calculated. His forehead bunched up slightly. "Yes. The test was positive all three times I had the lab run it."

Well, that would have been Riley's next question. Abbot had verified the test. So the results were almost certainly real. Tessa was pregnant.

Man, she was pregnant.

Despite the jolt of the news, Riley didn't have any trouble carrying that info through to the next step. Tessa had already admitted that it'd been months since she'd had sex, so that meant the child had been conceived during Fletcher's medical procedure.

During that insemination.

Riley took that through to the ultimate conclusion.

The child was his.

Her father pulled out the single stool tucked beneath the bar and sat down. "We need to talk about what happened in that clinic."

That didn't sound like the opening to good news that Riley figured they all needed right now. What little air he had managed to recoup, he lost again. He sank down onto the arm of the sofa and tried to brace himself for whatever Abbot was about to add.

"Thanks to surveillance video you recovered before the explosion, we were able to determine that Fletcher didn't tamper with any of the material he used during the insemination," Abbot explained.

"Material." A generic word for something that hadn't been generic.

"So, Riley is…"

That was as far as Tessa got.

She made another attempt, repeating those same three words, but then gave up and shook her head.

"The baby's mine," Riley said for her.

And he was damn glad he was sitting.

Powerful words indeed.

Life-changing words.

Words he thought he'd never hear himself say.

"*Our* baby," he corrected a moment later.

Abbot issued another of those crisp nods. "The surgery that Tessa had for the endometriosis was obviously successful after all."

"Obviously," Riley and she mumbled in unison.

Probably because her legs were about to give way, she sank down onto the floor and leaned her back against the sofa. She made another of those soft groans and buried her face in her hands.

"I know the timing for this question might seem too soon, especially since you haven't had a chance to discuss it, but as your mission commander, I have to ask." Abbot paused again. "What are your plans regarding this pregnancy?"

Riley held his breath.

Tessa pulled her hands from her face, slowly, and stared at her father. "I'll continue it, of course. There's no other option. Not for me."

Riley hadn't expected her to say otherwise. Tessa wanted a child, and it wouldn't matter to her that this was unexpected. She would still want this child.

Odd that he'd known that and her father hadn't.

"All right," Abbot finally said. But his resolute expression gave nothing away. If he had any opinion as to how he felt about his daughter's decision to make him a grandfather, he didn't show it. "There'll be paperwork. You'll need to get it started after we've resolved what we're going to do about Fletcher."

Even with everything else going on in his head, Riley didn't miss that. "What about Fletcher?"

"He's looking for info on the two of you." No pause or hesitation this time, which meant Abbot was probably more comfortable discussing a killer than Tessa's pregnancy. "He's also digging well beyond your cover identities. Well, at least he's trying to do that. He took your fingerprints, we believe, from the pen you used to sign the agreement, and he's having various labs run them for matches. In addition, he's distributing photographs."

Riley hadn't wanted to hear that. Especially now. Tessa and he already had enough to deal with, but apparently fate was about to dish out even more. "Clear photographs?"

"Clear enough. It appears he culled out some stills from the surveillance videos at the clinic. If he shows them to someone that either of you have worked with on a case, or even some casual contact who knows your real identities, then Fletcher could find you."

"We're in danger," Tessa concluded.

And because her voice trembled, because she was trembling, Riley moved down on the floor and put his arm around her.

"Not immediate danger," John Abbot assured them as he stood. "Your covers have held. At least I believe they have. But I'm placing a security operative in front of the condo to keep an eye on the place."

Riley knew that wasn't standard procedure. After all, Tessa and he were agents. Security operatives were for people who couldn't take care of themselves. Maybe Abbot was just being overly cautious.

If so, Riley would join him in that overly cautious status and stay alert.

Abbot took his keys from his pocket, but he didn't leave. He stood there a moment as if debating what he would say. "Tomorrow, I'd like the two of you to go to a safe house for a few days." He glanced at Riley. "In the meantime, I suppose you'd be willing to stay here? Temporarily, that is."

"I'm staying," Riley confirmed.

Tessa looked at him, as well. That *look* didn't exactly carry an engraved invitation with it, either.

"That's not up for negotiation," Riley assured her, just in case she was about to launch into an argument about being able to take care of herself.

"After we have security measures in place, I expect you to contact the chief," Abbot interjected, calling Riley's attention back to him. "For whatever disciplinary action he deems appropriate."

Riley didn't care what anyone deemed appropriate. Chiefs, disciplinary action and everything else would have to wait in line.

Right now, he had only one thing on his mind.

He needed to concentrate every ounce of his energy on keeping Tessa safe.

WITHIN SECONDS of her father's departure Riley got up from the floor, went to the door and locked it. He also reset the security system, even engaging the motion-detector lights for both the front and back of the condo. Tessa was sorry she hadn't thought of that first. But there was too much going on in her head for her to remember such things.

Not good, because it was a really bad time not to be vigilant.

Riley walked into the kitchen, rummaged through the cabinets until he located a glass and a bottle of Jack Daniel's. He poured himself a shot, a huge one, and downed it in one gulp. He made a sound. Half groan, half grunt. It had a ring of approval to it, so the drink must have accomplished its intended purpose.

"I'm sure you could use one," Riley commented, putting the bottle and glass away. "But under the circumstances, you should probably pass."

Because she was pregnant.

The one word pounded in her head. Definitely not a word she'd ever thought would apply to her. And yet, it not only applied, it created a whole new set of emotions and problems that Riley and she would have to deal with eventually.

Well, at least she'd have to deal with them.

She wasn't sure if Riley even fit into the picture. Again, this was new territory.

"Say something," she insisted, unable to make her voice louder than a whisper. "Anything."

"Anything, huh? Well, I can say with absolute certainty that this evening has been memorable." Riley went to her, reached down and scooped her up into his arms. "I want you to take that bubble bath you mentioned when you first got home, and then you can get some rest."

"You're dodging the issues, and that's not necessary. I'm not fragile, Riley."

"Oh, yes, you are. About this, anyway." He carried her through the doorway, deposited her on the foot of her bed, unzipped her boots and went into the adjoining bathroom so he could turn on the water in the tub. "You're allowed to be fragile. And you're allowed to be upset. Just because you've always wanted a baby, it doesn't mean you can't be distressed by the timing and by the surprise of it." He paused. "By the irony of it."

Yes. The irony. And what an irony it was.

She'd lost hope of ever having a child of her own, and yet a killer, the very man she was trying to stop, had given her the thing she wanted most.

True irony.

Of course, by giving her the baby, he'd thrown everything else into chaos. And drawn Riley into that chaos, as well. Because even though it would have been easier to dismiss this as her problem and hers alone, she couldn't.

It was, after all, Riley's child.

"Is this some kind of decorating trend that I haven't heard about?" Riley asked, tipping his head to the dead ficus near the linen closet.

She had to swallow the lump in her throat before she could speak. "It's my metaphorical attempt to put down roots. And you're changing the subject."

"You noticed that, huh?"

"I noticed."

And she wouldn't let him get away with it.

Riley opened a bottle of lavender bubble bath, sniffed it and gave a nod of approval. He poured at least six times too much into the tub. He motioned for her to undress and then made a show of clamping his hand over his eyes.

Yet another ironic gesture.

Here he was, preserving her modesty even though she was carrying his child. Of course, they hadn't taken the normal route for conception. The clinic insemination had done what would have normally happened through an intimate act.

Riley obviously wasn't going to let her opt out of the bubble bath, so Tessa began to shed her clothes. "I swore to you that it was okay for me to go through that insemination. You tried to talk me out of it, and I wouldn't listen."

"And your point would be?" he flatly asked.

"If I'd listened to you, if I'd talked Fletcher out of the procedure, we wouldn't be having this discussion. We wouldn't be in this situation."

"But you wouldn't have listened to me, now would you? A good thing, too. Because the mission would have been canceled before we could even go to the clinic, and we wouldn't be close to getting Fletcher."

It was a truly optimistic slant on things.

And it was pure BS.

There was no way Riley could be this undaunted by what they'd just learned. No way. While the appointment had indeed put them closer to apprehending Fletcher, the cost of that had been astronomical. Life-altering.

Naked, Tessa walked by him and stepped into the warm, bubbly water, even though she was certain the bath was yet another ploy to distract her.

"For the record, I don't believe most of what you just tossed out there, but it was the nice thing to say," she let Riley know. "The *right* thing."

"Blind luck, I assure you." He lowered his hand from his eyes, slowly, and when he saw that the bubbles had covered the majority of her body, he turned off the water and sat on the floor next to the tub. "We're both flying by the seat of our pants on this one, but we'll get through it."

He was so good at that. The right words. The right tone. Tessa had to look beyond the cool facade of those gray eyes and see all the concerns that she knew were there.

"You're allowed to be fragile, too, Riley."

The corner of his mouth lifted. For a second. Then he groaned and rubbed his hand over his face. "Okay, you're right. The idea of you being pregnant hasn't quite made it through my thick skull. And even if it had, it would have to share brain time with the fact that I'm scared that I won't be able to protect you."

Strange, she'd been thinking the same thing about him. "I'm not helpless," she reminded him.

"Neither was Colette, and Fletcher killed her."

Riley glanced in the general direction of her stomach. "And now the stakes are even higher."

Yes, they were.

Tessa didn't even try to deny that. She wasn't helpless, but she was vulnerable. Because if Fletcher harmed her, he would also harm her baby.

"Oh, God," she mumbled.

A half hour ago she hadn't even known a child existed. She hadn't even thought it possible.

And now, it effected everything.

Everything.

"It doesn't seem real," she admitted, shoving her hands through her hair. "Like I'm going to wake up and it's all going to be a dream."

He nodded. "I guess it'll take a while to get used to the idea."

An understatement. Eventually they'd have to figure out how they were going to handle all of this. No easy task, either. The possible solutions seemed as unreal as the test results.

When she'd thought she couldn't become pregnant, she had built her entire life around being an SIU agent. All in all, it was a good substitute, one she'd learned to cherish nearly as much as she would have a child.

Nearly.

And her devotion to duty had been the one thing that her father had noticed.

Not her.

Only the job.

And the job was the very thing this pregnancy could jeopardize.

She slipped deeper into the water, hoping the heat and fragrance would loosen her stiff muscles. It wouldn't, of course. But then, nothing could do that.

"You're sighing," Riley pointed out.

"Am I?" Tessa went back through her most recent responses and realized it was true. "You've done your share of that tonight."

He made a humph sound. "Real men don't sigh. We just ponder and brood while making manly grunting noises."

Tessa slipped her gaze in his direction. "You're trying to cheer me up."

"Yeah. Is it working?"

She sighed again.

Riley flexed his eyebrows. "Guess not." Using his thumb and index finger, he thumped one of the bubbles, bursting it.

Tessa closed her eyes a moment. Not to relax. That wouldn't happen tonight. But it seemed a good time to ask what she figured was a rhetorical question. "What are the odds of this happening anyway?"

"Pretty good, actually. Fletcher obviously knew from your medical info that the timing was perfect for you to conceive a child."

Since Riley answered so quickly, that meant he'd probably already given this some thought. It made Tessa wonder what else he had thought about. What was he feeling? And was he as poleaxed as she was?

No doubt.

"Fletcher moved up the insemination because he knew you were ovulating," Riley continued. "That, and because he wanted to make sure he kept the element of surprise."

"Well, he managed the surprise part. We created a baby without ever having had sex."

"Right." He paused. "One of the advantages of modern technology."

Tessa frowned at the glib way he dismissed that. Judging from his somber expression, he was experiencing no such glibness. "At least I've had some incredibly intense pleasurable moments normally associated with becoming pregnant." She shrugged. "Even though those moments came after the fact. You haven't even had that."

He laughed, but it was mixed with a full dose of weariness. "Was that a pass?" He turned to look at her. "Or are you just rubbing it in?"

She touched his arm. She had to feel his warmth. His body. Him. "It would have been a pass if I had the energy to do something about it."

He moved closer. "That's the other thing about men. We always have the energy *to do something about it.*"

But instead of giving her a hot kiss that would have initiated foreplay and bathtub sex—something she was sure she would have found the energy to do—Riley gently cupped her chin and brushed his mouth over her cheek. The chaste gesture only confirmed that he was going through his own personal version of torture.

"Will you tell your parents?" Tessa asked and wasn't surprised that she was afraid to hear his answer. The photos in his personnel file flashed in her head. His father. His mother. People he still had a connection to. And they were also people who had been pulled into this simply because of a DNA connection.

"Sure. Eventually. I mean, they'll need to know. Especially since your father knows." And with that, Riley gave a loud, manly sigh.

"I'm sorry," Tessa said.

"Don't. We're not going through that, because this isn't our fault. Not yours. Not mine. It's not as if we had wild, unprotected sex." He glanced at her. "Even though if any more of those bubbles pop, I just might haul your naked body out of that tub—"

A clicking sound stopped him from finishing that.

Riley's gaze flew to the doorway, just as the outside light slashed through her otherwise dark bedroom.

"The motion detector," she whispered.

Someone had tripped it.

Chapter Eleven

Tessa stilled. Listening.

And praying.

Praying that the sound she heard wasn't an indication that someone had just breached the perimeter security of her condo.

But her instincts screamed that was exactly what had happened.

Riley's instincts were obviously right there with hers because he tossed her a towel. "Get dressed," he whispered. It was definitely an order. One she didn't need because Tessa already understood what might be happening.

Pulling the weapon from the shoulder holster beneath his leather jacket, Riley crawled across the tiled floor, reached up and slapped off the light switch. The sudden darkness only accentuated the outside lights spilling into her bedroom. The lights were by the French doors that led to her tiny backyard and patio. The only way they would have been triggered was for someone to be on the property.

And right at her back door.

Tessa stepped from the tub. She didn't bother to dry off, even though she felt the soapy water slide down her body and onto the floor. Staying low, Riley crawled into her bedroom, snagged the clothes she'd left on the bed and tossed them to her.

She peeked around the door frame and tried to get a feel for what was happening. The gauzy white curtains covering the doors made it impossible to see outside, so she watched for shadows. For any sign of movement.

For anything.

She saw nothing, but there was another sound. Soft. Maybe a footstep.

Maybe not.

A sound so faint that any other time Tessa might have dismissed it as nothing. Especially since this was her home.

She pulled on her jeans and top, then hit the floor and scurried to her nightstand where she retrieved the 9 mm handgun she kept there. While she was at it, she got some extra magazines of ammo and stuffed them into her pockets. She could only hope that she wouldn't need them, but that sense of dread that had taken hold of her stomach told her otherwise.

"Find out if that's your father's security specialist out there," Riley insisted, his voice barely audible. "And if it's not, request backup."

Still crouching, Tessa reached for the phone next to her bed.

Reaching for it was as far as she got.

One of the doors suddenly shattered. A loud burst set off the security alarm and sent shards of glass spewing across the room.

Tessa instinctively ducked, using her bed for cover and sheltering her eyes from the dangerous debris. But her instincts didn't keep her behind cover for long. She came up ready to fire.

So did Riley.

In all probability, the person responsible wasn't an SIU security specialist. It was an intruder, probably sent by Fletcher. And that meant he had not only learned who they were, he knew where to find them. Their cover had failed to hold. Fletcher had broken through all those carefully erected layers that had sheltered them.

Riley and she waited, braced to deal with whatever came through the gaping hole in the door.

No one came.

The ghost-white curtains fluttered in the night breeze, stirring toward the bed, and the strangling silence closed in around them.

With each passing second Tessa's adrenaline surged. Her heart pounded. Her muscles knotted. All normal reactions that she'd experienced every time she'd been in danger.

However, there were new reactions, as well.

Amid all of those responses came thoughts of the pregnancy. Dangerous thoughts, because this wasn't the time to focus on anything but the intruder. Or more likely, *intruders*. Fletcher would have almost certainly sent a team of gunmen and not a single operative to kill them.

With his attention fastened to the French doors, Riley motioned for her to go into the living room. Tessa hesitated. Not because it wasn't a smart thing to do.

It was.

It would get her out of the line of fire, but it would also leave Riley in danger. Plus, she wouldn't be able to back him up if anyone rushed the room.

"You're coming, too," she whispered.

And she made sure it wasn't a request.

Riley motioned again and mumbled some profanity under his breath. With her gun still cocked and locked, she inched away from the nightstand, behind Riley, until she was side by side with him.

He shot her a disapproving glare, but Tessa didn't budge. She wouldn't leave him to fight this fight alone.

"Think of the baby," he whispered.

The impact of the words nearly knocked the breath out of her. He couldn't have said anything else that would have forced her to rethink all her training. To push aside what had become second nature.

But that did it.

Because this wasn't just about her, or her need to back up a fellow agent. The baby was part of this now. And if Fletcher's henchmen succeeded in hurting her, then, they would also succeed in hurting the baby.

Suddenly the child she carried inside her wasn't some vague notion to be dealt with later. Not some test that she'd taken during a routine physical. And not some moneymaking scam devised by a killer. It was real. A tiny life that she was responsible for.

Oh, God.

"Get moving," Riley ordered.

Tessa did. Because she had no other choice, she did.

While still trying to provide Riley with some measure of cover, she eased back. Slowly. Trying not to make a sound. She crawled toward the doorway that separated her bedroom from the living room.

A gust of wind, or something, caught the curtain and the limp fabric snapped like a bullwhip. Tessa didn't let it distract her. Which was a good thing, because she finally saw a shadowy figure on her patio.

A man.

He had a gun.

That image barely had time to register when the next shot slammed through the wall just above her head. It was quickly followed by another.

Then another.

Until it was nonstop.

It was a barrage of deadly gunfire that was aimed right at Riley and her.

Tessa dropped all the way to the floor. But she didn't stay put, she couldn't. She was literally blocking Riley's exit, and the bed would give him no protection whatsoever against those bullets.

Repositioning her gun so she could return fire, she dove to the side, came up on one knee. Tessa squeezed the trigger, her own shots tearing through what was left of the curtains and the French doors. It was a risk. Because each shot that she took meant there was a chance she'd hit an innocent bystander.

Or else *she* could be hit.

Still, she had to try to stop what these assassins had set into motion.

With her other hand, she latched onto Riley. Grappling to cover each other, they maneuvered. Repositioned. Until somehow, they made it into the living room.

Gunfire pelted the condo. Bullets tore through the walls and penetrated the interior. Not simple handguns. Not this. Whoever was shooting at them was using automatics. Nor was it just one gunman. The pattern of the shots indicated at least two shooters. Maybe three. In other words, they'd likely come to kill and didn't care how much spare ammunition they had to use to get the job done.

Or how much attention they attracted.

"The front motion detector light isn't on," she relayed to Riley.

It was a little good news at a time when they could really use some. It meant the assassins weren't out front.

Well, maybe that's what it meant.

There was a possibility they were out there but had purposely stayed back so they wouldn't trip the motion detector and alert them. If so, they were probably waiting for Riley and her to come running through the door.

In other words, a trap.

Unfortunately that door and the window in the dining area were the only exits, their only hope of getting out of this alive.

She picked through the noise of the security alarms and listened to the pattern of the gunfire. All the shots were still concentrated on the rear of the building. Not gunfire from weapons rigged with silencers, either. Which meant one of her neighbors had almost certainly called the cops by now. It also meant the security specialist that her father had positioned somewhere outside was likely dead. Murdered. If he were still alive, she would have heard the sounds of someone trying to return fire.

That was the bad news.

But as bad as it was, it didn't mean Riley and she could stay put. The approaching sounds of police sirens might scare off the assassins, but if they were truly determined, and it appeared that they were, then they'd just kill the officers and continue with their deadly mission. So, to save themselves and possibly others, Riley and she had no choice but to move fast.

Riley must have come to the same conclusion. "We're going out the window," he said over the din of the gunfire and the security alarm.

It was the exit route she would have chosen. Now, she only hoped his concurrence meant it was their best chance of getting out alive.

Tessa followed Riley's lead. Or rather, she tried. But he pushed her in front of him so that he'd be the one in the line of fire. Normally, Tessa would have *objected* to such kid-glove treatment. But this wasn't normal. Under the circumstances, she was thankful that Riley's first concern was protecting their child, because it had become a major concern of hers.

They crawled across the floor, together, and when they reached the dining room window, Riley traded places with her, putting himself at the most dangerous point of impact. He opened the window, knocked out the screen with his elbow. Glanced out. And quickly ducked back into the meager cover.

"It looks clear," he said. "But we can't use your

car. They might have rigged it with explosives. We'll have to leave on foot."

Tessa nodded. Being on foot would make them easier targets, but he was right. Her car had been parked out front for nearly an hour. Anyone could have gotten to it.

"On the count of three," he said. "One…"

Still staying low, Tessa shifted so she could spring to her feet and start running.

"Two." But she didn't actually hear him say the word because of another round of deafening gunfire.

"Three."

Riley launched himself through the window, landing on his feet on the grassy area outside. With his weapon ready, he stopped. Aimed. Looked around to make sure it was safe and then motioned for her to follow.

Tessa did, and the moment her feet touched the ground, they began to run. Following the building and using it for cover, Riley led her behind a row of hedges until they reached the last unit in the complex. He didn't pause. Didn't waste even a second of time.

"Go!" he ordered in a hoarse whisper.

They raced out into the darkness, toward the side street. And away from her home. Away from the one place that she'd thought of as her sanctuary.

But no longer.

There was no sanctuary. No real place to hide. Because as long as Fletcher was alive, he would continue to come after them.

And that meant he would continue to put their child in harm's way.

WHILE HE TRIED to keep a close watch behind them, Riley led Tessa out of the alley and zigzagged around several more buildings until he came to another street.

Things didn't look good.

After a thirty-minute jog that he'd kept semilight for Tessa's sake, they'd made it away from her neighborhood and from the gunman. But now they were no longer in one of the best sections of the city.

And there wasn't a taxi in sight.

Not that it surprised Riley, but it was more than a mild inconvenience. It was too dangerous to try to get back to his car, which he'd parked a block from Tessa's condo, and he didn't want to risk breaking into one of the vehicles parked along the street. Still, he couldn't just stand here with Tessa. Those gunmen could be in pursuit.

Keeping in the shadows as much as they could, they made their way up the sidewalk. Riley continued to study the street and the buildings. And he continued to think, to assess their situation, the gunmen and the attack itself.

He didn't care much for the conclusions he came to from that assessment.

"Fletcher would have insisted his henchmen surround your condo," he mumbled.

"Yes." No hesitation, which meant Tessa had come to the same conclusion. "But if that was a ploy to follow us, I haven't seen anyone."

Neither had he. So the ploy could have failed.

Could have.

Or maybe Fletcher's men were just very good at tracking. Maybe they were using sophisticated equipment instead of a pursuit on foot. Or maybe they'd been overly confident of their abilities to gain access through the French doors and kill Tessa and him on the spot.

Since Riley wasn't sure he'd have answers to that anytime soon and because it was stupid to keep Tessa out in the open any longer, he headed for the small two-story hotel that he saw a block ahead. He thanked his lucky stars that no one passed them along the way.

"Where are we going?" she whispered.

Riley didn't answer. Instead he gave her a warning glance to stay quiet and stepped inside the hotel. The burly desk clerk barely glanced up from his wrestling magazine, and there was no interest whatsoever in his dull raisin-colored eyes. Riley took some cash from his pocket, slapped it on the counter and requested a room on the second floor. He had the key card for Room 212 within seconds.

Which he didn't use.

Instead Tessa and he made their way down the hall and he tapped on the door of Room 214. No answer, just as he'd hoped. But then, it didn't look like a place that got a lot of business on a late Thursday evening.

He used one of the small tools he always carried to jimmy the lock and got them inside. Hopefully, being in the room meant some degree of safety, but he didn't intend to rely on the rickety door and the desk clerk to keep out any pursuing gunmen. No, he'd have to do that himself.

Thankfully, the interior wasn't quite as bad as the outside of the building. Still, it was basically a site he couldn't secure, a realization that made him silently curse both the surroundings and the situation that had put them here.

How the devil had he let this happen?

With Tessa's help, Riley dragged the dresser in front of the door, blocking it, then he lifted a corner of the curtains to look out at the sidewalk below. No one either walking or driving by.

"I don't want to use normal channels to contact headquarters," he insisted.

"I know. There might be a leak in communication."

Riley confirmed that with a nod. "Fletcher found us. Fast. If his goons had tracked us through the woods the day the clinic exploded, then they would have hit sooner. Much sooner."

"I see your point." She sank down onto the edge of the bed. "So you think the leak is someone in SIU?"

"Possibly. Money can be a powerful incentive. And the betrayal wouldn't have necessarily come from an agent. In fact, I suspect it didn't. Fletcher wouldn't have wanted to take that kind of risk. Instead he probably went after a clerk, someone with just enough info for him to be able to put the pieces together to find you."

Since the gunmen went to Tessa's condo, Fletcher might have intended to *question* her so they could then find him. Or maybe, just maybe, the gunmen had followed him and waited until after he'd broken in and Tessa had arrived.

A thought that sickened Riley.

Because he could have been the one to lead the gunmen right to Tessa.

The pregnancy put her in a weak position, which was especially true because he knew how much having a baby meant to her. Despite the shock of it all, this child was her miracle, and somehow, some way, he had to get her out of Fletcher's path so her miracle wouldn't turn into another nightmare.

He knew Tessa wouldn't appreciate his intervention. Well, not at first anyway. She wouldn't want him taking the brunt of the danger so he could keep her safe. But the pregnancy wasn't just a vulnerability. Riley could use it for leverage. Leverage to make her stay hidden safely away while he went after Fletcher.

And that was exactly what he would do.

What he *had* to do.

This wasn't a Boy Scout outing where playing by the rules counted. Nothing counted except saving Tessa and making Fletcher pay for all the things he'd done.

Tessa blew out a long breath. "How does all of this affect the trip to the art gallery in Houston?"

Good question. While they were running for their lives, it had actually crossed Riley's mind. "That painting is the only direct link I have to Fletcher. It's my key to finding him."

"It's also his key to finding you," she pointed out. "Think this through, Riley. Fletcher might suspect we're coming. He'll know the art was mentioned on the tape. Heck, he might have even used it to set us up. Our only advantage is that he doesn't actually know we have the tape."

All logical points. But she'd missed the most important point of all. "There's no *we* in this, Tessa. There can't be. I can't take you with me."

And just in case she didn't grasp the point he was making, he placed his hand against her stomach.

Riley had intended the gesture to be an exclamation point to his demand. For some strange reason, it seemed a lot more than that. One touch, one brief brush of his fingers on her stomach, and it became his own exclamation point.

A reminder that this pregnancy affected both of them on many levels.

Her mouth tightened and Tessa moved his hand away. "What are you saying, that it's safer for me to stay here while you're out there trying to track Fletcher down by yourself?"

Riley skipped right over that last part—especially since there was a very good chance he'd have to do it alone. Because of that possible breach in security, he couldn't trust SIU with this, and it was too dangerous to take Tessa with him.

"You won't be here by yourself," he let her know. "I'll call your father so he can stay with you."

She groaned. "And what about the leak? Someone at SIU headquarters could listen in on your conversation."

"I'll contact him at home so I won't have to go through SIU channels." Riley leaned closer and got right in her face so she could hopefully see the determination in his eyes. "Now, you think it through. I need someone we can trust. Someone that Fletcher can't buy off with his millions. And just as important,

I need someone to watch out for you in case Fletcher finds this place."

Because he was staring into her own determined eyes, he saw that register. By degrees. A fraction at a time. Until a frustrated sigh left her mouth. "This isn't fair to you. We're in danger because of *our* mission, because of what happened in that clinic. Yet, you'll have to face the danger alone."

Riley silently disagreed with that *fair* part of her argument. In the grand cosmic scheme of things, this was as fair as it got. It was exactly what he deserved. He hadn't been there to save Colette. She'd died while he was tucked safely away in a surveillance van.

Protecting Tessa wouldn't undo that.

It couldn't.

But it could go a long way to making him feel as if there'd been some retribution. Some justice. Some healing. Of course, the retribution and justice would be complete only if he brought down Fletcher in the process.

Riley moved away from her and went back to the window so he could keep watch. And so he wouldn't let the haunting look in Tessa's eyes distract him. In a few hours, before John Abbot left for work, he'd call and ask the man to come and stay with Tessa. Once that was in place, then Riley would leave for

Houston. A journey that would eventually make things safe for Tessa.

And for the child that she carried.

His child.

Because no matter how hard he fought to keep Tessa and the baby from causing him to lose focus, they did. They were both right there, piercing his thoughts and tearing into his concentration.

And that made both their situations all the more dangerous.

Chapter Twelve

The sound of someone talking woke Tessa.

It was Riley. He was whispering, his voice barely audible. That captured her attention almost as quickly as if he'd been shouting.

She sat up in bed, suddenly frustrated that she'd fallen asleep.

And even more frustrated that he obviously hadn't.

Tessa glanced at the clock next to the bed. It was nearly 3:00 a.m. Riley was still by the window, keeping watch. Probably the only time he'd left that sentry position was to pull the covers over her. Strange that she hadn't recalled him doing that. Normally a movement of any kind would have brought her out of a deep sleep.

He glanced at her and continued the conversation on his cell phone. His responses were brief and clipped. *No. Yes.* Another *yes.* It was only after he added a *sir,* that Tessa confirmed he was talking to her father.

"She's awake," Riley told him. And with that, he passed the phone to her. "He wants to talk to you."

"Tessa," her father said when she answered. "Riley just gave me a situation report on the shooting. We have an evidence response team at your place now. If the gunmen left anything behind, we'll find it."

Tessa was positive the only evidence would be shell casings, and Fletcher would have made sure those couldn't be traced.

"I'll have another team en route to your specified location within ten minutes," her father continued. "They won't be told that Riley and you are there, only that it's an area that needs to be purged and secured. I anticipate that'll be completed by 0500."

Soon. Very soon. A little over two hours. Not much time, and in some ways, it seemed an eternity.

"Are you…all right?" her father asked.

She opened her mouth. Closed it. And briefly wondered why that question seemed so awkward. Then she realized it was a first. In the seven years she'd been an SIU agent, he'd never asked that. Never.

"I'm fine," she lied.

"Good." She heard no breath of relief. No relief of any kind, but she thought maybe it was there just beneath the surface. "I'll contact you after the area is secure."

Tessa clicked off the phone and handed it to Riley. "What made you decide to ask for a security team?"

"I didn't." He slipped his phone back into his jacket pocket. "I didn't tell your father the truth."

Her head whipped up. "But he said he was sending a team to the specified location."

"It's the *specified* part that isn't true. I gave him a false location on the west side of the city."

Certain that her mouth was gaping a bit, she stared at him. "What, now you don't trust him?"

"I trust him. I don't trust a team, any team. One of them could be the leak. Or else Fletcher could be monitoring SIU headquarters to tail any personnel who comes out of the building. This way, if Fletcher has the place under surveillance, your father's team won't lead them right to us."

Okay. She saw his point and was more than mildly annoyed that he'd had to explain it to her. Mercy, she should have already anticipated a contingency like that.

"So where does that leave us?" she asked. "Certainly we aren't just going to sit here and wait."

"In an hour I'll call your father again. Once he's sure no one is following him, he'll come here to stay with you."

It was a good plan, and probably would have seemed even better if she'd had a more active part in it. "And you'll leave for Houston."

"I'll leave for Houston," he verified.

So they didn't have much time. A couple of hours at the most.

"If Fletcher manages to find us and if he can get the hotel clerk to tell him where we are, we'll hear his henchmen going into the next room," Riley assured her. He stood and began to pace. What he didn't do was take his attention from the window. He continued to volley glances in that direction. "I haven't seen anyone suspicious on the sidewalk or street. It's not a guarantee of safety, but it's the best we can do under the circumstances."

Tessa nodded. She also took note of the concern that was all over Riley's face. The concern was warranted, of course, but during their entire stay with Fletcher, she hadn't seen him react this way. "Maybe this is a good time to reiterate that pregnancy hormones won't affect my shooting ability. Or my common sense. If Fletcher gets through, I know how to take care of myself."

"Is that your way of telling me not to worry?" He stopped pacing and eased down next to her on the bed. "If so, it won't do any good. I'll still worry."

Of course, he would. Part of this was the leftover effect of Colette's murder. Heck, maybe it was totally from that. But then, that would mean Riley didn't care about her.

And Tessa didn't believe that.

She didn't *want* to believe it.

The kisses they'd shared, the incident in her condo, weren't all just lust. There was a lot more to what was happening between them.

He leaned down, pressed his ear to her stomach. Turned. And then brushed a kiss there. It was a strange, intimate gesture that suddenly didn't feel so strange. It felt...right.

"Are you going to be part of this?" she asked.

"I'm already part of this."

Not exactly the grand declaration of fatherhood, but she hadn't expected it from him. Riley was no doubt still coming to terms with the pregnancy.

As was she.

He made his way up to her mouth and gave her a quick, almost chaste kiss. "You're thinking too much."

"There's a lot to think about," she countered.

He made a sound of agreement and for a moment Tessa thought they were about to have that heart-to-heart they so desperately needed to have. But then he kissed her again. Not just an ordinary kiss, either. It was one that involved some readjusting. Repositioning. And a slick move or two that had her wondering if the world had just tipped on its axis.

Riley eased her back, until her head landed on the pillow.

He pulled back, stared into her eyes, and one of those *manly* troubled groans left his mouth.

Tessa touched her fingertips to his forehead to

massage the muscles that had bunched there. "I thought you said we weren't the missionary or the bed type."

He smiled. Short-lived, though. "I'm flexible. Besides, this isn't going any further than a kiss. Well, maybe we can stretch it into a French kiss and a few touches. Afterward though, I want you to rest until your father gets here."

"You're the one who needs the rest. I'm not traveling to Houston to pursue a killer. I'll be stuck in a safe house, and the operative words there are 'stuck' and 'safe.'"

Something that Riley wouldn't be.

That sent a sickening feeling of dread through her. Tessa shifted, maneuvering him until he was the one lying on the bed. She started to climb around him, with the intentions of going to the window to keep watch, but Riley caught her arm.

"I've tried to think of all the scenarios where Fletcher might be able to draw you out into the open," Riley said, his voice strained. "He's smart, and the only thing he wants is us dead. You can't let him draw you out. No matter what."

Now it was Tessa's turn to give him a chaste, reassuring kiss on the cheek. "I know what you've been through with Colette—"

"This has nothing to do with her." He hesitated a moment. "In some ways it'd be easier if it did. If I could tie all of it up into a neat little package where my feelings are based on revenge and duty."

Riley's gaze came to hers again and Tessa waited. Long, quiet moments. Practically holding her breath to see how much more he would open up to her. But he didn't speak. He reached up, slid his hand around the back of her neck and eased her down toward him.

He kissed her.

Not chaste. Not this. Nor was it exactly a kiss of heated, raw passion. It was filled with so much need, so much emotion, that it poured through her. All through her. Until it seemed as if he'd shared his heart, his body and every nuance of himself with her. This was more intimate, more frightening, than what they'd done in her condo.

She almost pulled back. Almost retreated. But Riley didn't give her the chance. He pulled her closer. Not quickly, either. A slow movement with their gazes still locked.

The only light came from the street and filtered through the curtains. It was enough, more than enough, for her to see in his eyes what he'd left unsaid. The questions. The doubts. The fears. And, yes, even the pain that would perhaps always be there.

Maybe then it would have ended. The embrace. The kiss. The long, lingering look. If only Tessa hadn't decided that she wouldn't let it end.

Maybe this was it. Maybe this was all they'd ever have, but if so, she wasn't ready to let go of it just yet.

"Tessa," he warned.

"Shh." And she brought that sound directly to his lips. To kiss him the way she wanted to kiss him.

His mouth was warm. Slightly rough. And already so familiar. As if his taste were somehow programmed into her DNA. A sensual trigger to make her body soften, make her blood race.

To make her feel as if he were the man she'd always wanted.

Perhaps he was.

Because Tessa was sure she'd never felt anything quite like this before.

She kissed him. Really kissed him. Letting their tongues meet. Taking his mouth as if it were hers for the taking. She took everything he was offering her. And everything that he wasn't.

Everything.

She felt herself go moist and damp, her body preparing for what his kiss had promised. And there was a lot of promise in that kiss.

He tried to move again, but Tessa stopped him. Holding him in place with her own body, pinning him to the bed, she pushed up his black T-shirt, exposing his chest and stomach. Finally she pulled the garment over his head and tossed it onto the floor.

Firm, flexing muscles, naturally tanned skin and

great abs. Not a perfect body but much more interesting than perfect—from the light sprinkling of dark chest hair, to the faint scar on his left forearm, to the other scar on his stomach. To a small dragon tattoo on his right shoulder blade.

Yes, a tattoo.

She ran her fingers over it and had the thrill of hearing him suck in his breath.

"A relic from a weekend in Singapore," he murmured with some difficulty. Perhaps because she was still stroking that tattoo and then slid her fingers through his chest hair. Barely touching, with just her fingertips. "A *drunken* weekend," he added.

The thought of him drunk and not in control made her smile. It also made her have some very evil thoughts of doing whatever it took to push him over the edge. Of course, she, too, would enjoy that pushing as much as he did.

"Should I be afraid?" Riley asked, grumbling softly when she moved her fingers to trace the outline of his left nipple.

"Definitely."

Even half-naked, he had that bad-boy image down pat. Desperado stubble on his chin. That I-dare-you look in his smoky-gray eyes. His mouth, still wet from their kisses. And it really didn't surprise Tessa to realize that she had a sudden yearning to put her hands on Riley and all that badness.

The heat rolled through her.

She leaned in and took his mouth again, and she felt it all the way to her stomach when he made a deep male sound of satisfaction and pleasure. She eased all the way on top of him. Aligning their bodies. Until she felt the solid muscles of his chest against her breasts. Felt the sinewy strength of his arms.

She especially felt his erection.

And in that moment Tessa knew exactly what she would do with Riley McDade.

"Be afraid," she whispered, teasing. "Be very afraid."

RILEY DIDN'T EVEN TRY to pull back. Didn't even try to remember why this wasn't a good idea.

Something clicked. Something primal. Something deep within him. And he knew any resistance that he could attempt would fail.

Her scent was all around him. Covering him. Drowning him. Yet he wanted more of her. He wanted all of her.

She turned slightly. Her loose top slid off her shoulder, exposing the right cup of her white bra. And exposing the top of her breast. It was a reminder he'd never actually seen her bare breasts. Or kissed them. In her condo, he'd simply touched her and nothing more.

He did something about that.

Yanking off her top, he unclipped the front closure on her bra and had the satisfaction of her breasts spilling out into his hands. She was small. Firm.

Perfect.

The sight of her, of her pale skin in the milky light, was nearly his undoing.

Man, she was beautiful.

He skimmed his hand over her breasts. Just enough to make her nipples tighten. Just enough to make her arch her back and thrust her body closer. Riley took her up on that nonverbal offer. He levered himself up and nipped her right nipple with his teeth. Not hard. But it was enough to make her moan softly. Since he liked the way that sound shaped her mouth, he did it again.

And again.

Tessa evidently liked the sensation because she immediately began to fight with his clothes. She went after his zipper. Her hands, hurrying.

And she failed.

Only because he went after hers first. Basically he played dirty and outmuscled her. She grappled with him, and just when he thought he might lose, he played even dirtier and took her nipple into his mouth.

"Oh," Tessa said.

Just "oh." Breathy. Needy. With a few extra syllables added to it. It was everything he wanted to hear. And it was just enough of a distraction that he got her zipper down and peeled the jeans right off her. While he was at it, he took off her bra, as well, leaving her with just a pair of flimsy white panties.

Riley took a moment to savor and appreciate the view.

Until Tessa did some dirty playing of her own. She slid her hand over the front of his jeans. That was certainly the way to get his attention. The fastest way, actually. It was a not-so-subtle move that had Riley going from seriously aroused to rock hard.

She tackled his zipper again, and this time she succeeded. He succeeded, as well, and got her out of those panties, the only barrier left between his hand and her.

He moved his fingers down her stomach and between her legs. He touched. Lightly. Testing her response and learning what she liked in the process. He slid his fingers across the sensitive little bud, slipped his index finger in even deeper and heard her say a very naughty word.

He touched her again, his finger going deeper until he found an even more sensitive spot. Meeting his gaze head-on, she rocked against his hand. A long, lingering caress that brought on another *oh,* another erotic hitch of her breath. And he was sure he had her close to release.

He was wrong.

"Not this time," she insisted. Tessa located his

mouth again, kissing him as if it were a life-and-death matter. "I'm not going alone."

And she obviously meant it.

Frantically she caught the waist of his jeans. Tugging and trying to rip them off him.

"Now," she insisted.

With his help, his boots and jeans came off, and when she had him naked and lying beneath her, she arched her back like a cat and slid her hands slowly over his chest. Her fingers gliding through the sweat that had already beaded on his skin.

She snared his gaze. Gave their bodies a necessary adjustment. No fumbling. She got it right the first time. But she gave him one last dirty playing shot by skimming the sweet heat of her body right over his erection.

Not once.

But multiple times.

Until Riley was sure he'd soon have to beg for mercy.

And only then did she take him inside her. By degrees. An inch at a time. Until she had taken all of him.

Tessa paused a moment. Maybe to catch her breath. Maybe to savor the moment. Riley was certainly doing some savoring and breath-catching of his own.

Bracketing her hands on his chest, she began to move. Slowly at first. Then faster. And faster. No frantic rhythm. But each move calculated. Precise. Each time sliding the moist heat of her body over the entire length of him.

Her unique scent and taste lingered around him and made him crazy.

A long, deliberate sigh left her mouth. A moan. And a gasp of pleasure. Once again she moved in an ancient rhythm. And she moved against him.

Deeper this time.

So deep.

She took him. Claimed him. And sent them both spiraling out of control. But out of control was the only place Riley wanted to go.

And he wanted Tessa to take him there.

With their blood raging. Face-to-face. Body-to-body. Wet skin whispering against wet skin. Him, inside her. Her, moving. Clutching. Gripping. Sliding. To a frantic, feverish pace that built and built and built until it was no longer just pleasure. But a necessity.

"Come with me," he managed to say.

She drove her body over him one last time. One last thrust. Until neither had a choice.

They slipped into that spiral together and surrendered.

Chapter Thirteen

"A relic from a drunken weekend in Singapore?" Tessa mumbled, running her fingertips over the dragon tattoo on Riley's shoulder.

The man was certainly interesting in many ways, and the fact that he was lying stark-naked beneath her allowed her complete access to all those interesting things.

Riley confirmed that tattoo question with a grunt. "Disgusting, huh?"

"No. Oddly, I find it…well, the opposite of disgusting." Tessa chuckled when he did. "It suits you and that whole bad-boy persona."

"It's supposed to be sort of a family crest. Supposedly, the ancient McDade warriors would strip off their clothes, paint their bodies blue and charge into battle." He flexed his eyebrows. "Not my first choice of ways to fight. A little too vulnerable, if you ask me. But I guess it worked for them. After all, their DNA survived and I'm here sporting their tattoo."

She stiffened at that last comment, because it reminded her of his genetic contribution to the child inside her. It also reminded her of the battle he had ahead of him.

Riley must have sensed her reaction because he skimmed his finger down her cheek. "Don't worry. There's not too much of a criminal faction in my DNA."

Tessa shook her head. "That's not what I'm worried about. It's everything else."

"Yes." He took a deep breath, glanced at the clock, and what was left of the light moment faded. "I need to call your father."

Tessa took a deep breath of her own and eased off him. "There's no reason I can't be the one to talk to him."

"Ditto," Riley countered. "He won't be pleased that we didn't tell him the truth up front and he'll want to *voice* his displeasure."

Not that she needed such a reminder. No, her father wouldn't care for the lie. Nor would he like the fact that she would certainly defend Riley's decision to withhold the truth from him.

"Ditto right back at you," Tessa said, forcing herself away from him. "You're bearing the brunt of the danger on this mission. The least I can do is handle the friendly fire of my father's wrath."

She hurriedly dressed, and while Riley was still putting on his jeans, she decided to make the call before he could resume the argument.

"It's me," Tessa said when her father picked up on the first ring.

No warm greetings. No more questions about her well-being. "You're not at the location Riley specified," he practically snarled.

"No." And Tessa chose her words carefully. "It's a security precaution."

Silence. For several long moments. "I hope that's not your way of saying you don't trust me."

Now it was time for some major damage control. "We trust you. *I* trust you. But we were afraid that Fletcher had SIU headquarters under surveillance."

Her father mumbled something she didn't even want to interpret. "Even if Fletcher had managed to do that, the team I sent out would have been careful."

"It isn't just the team," Tessa countered. "Riley and I thought there might be a leak and that maybe that's how Fletcher was able to identify me and send those gunmen to my place."

More silence. Then more mumblings. Somewhere in those mumblings, though, Tessa thought perhaps she heard her father concede a little.

"I'll do a thorough scan," her father promised. "If there's a leak, it'll show up."

"Thanks. And in case you didn't catch that, it was

a real thanks, not one of those obligatory things I'd say to my mission commander."

"You're welcome." He paused again. "And in case you didn't catch that, it wasn't obligatory, either. I mean it."

Tessa took a moment to savor that. Coming from her father, it was almost as good as saying I love you. Almost. So Tessa pushed it just a little further. "You did a good job raising me, Dad. I don't think I've ever told you thanks for that. But thanks."

He didn't have quite the reaction she'd expected. He cursed. "Is this your way of saying you don't think you're going to make it out of this situation?"

"No. I just wanted you to know."

"Believe me, I know. I also know you're one of the best on my team, but that doesn't make you invincible. Remember that. And stay safe."

"I will," she promised, and wasn't surprised to feel the hot tears in her eyes. Since it wasn't a good time for those, she added, "I think Riley needs to talk to you, as well." Blinking back those tears, she passed the cell phone to him.

"Yes, sir," Riley said a few seconds later. "It was a necessary precaution as far as I'm concerned."

Her father was no doubt revoicing his obligatory disapproval about the lie and about being kept out of the information loop.

"I need some supplies, transportation," Riley insisted. "And some backup."

Riley provided the name and the address of the art gallery in Houston, and Tessa listened as he requested the necessary agents and equipment. Not simply for surveillance but for possible apprehension or even tracking and pursuit of a dangerous suspect. It wasn't foolproof. Things could still go wrong. But at least Riley wasn't going after Fletcher alone. Tessa would remember that and thank him for it later. When the storm had passed.

When things were safe again.

The next bit of information that Riley provided was the address of the hotel where they were staying, and he did that only seconds before hanging up.

"Your father says he'll be here in fifteen minutes," Riley relayed to her. "No team, not for this one. Too risky."

It was equally risky for Riley to rely on a team in Houston, but Tessa didn't voice that. He knew what was at stake. So did she. And no matter how this mission progressed, the danger was still there.

The only way for the danger to stop was for them to find Fletcher.

That was her cue to put on her shoes and make sure she was ready to face her father. One glance in the mirror, though, and she realized there wasn't much she could do to erase the signs that she'd just made love to Riley. Her lips were slightly swollen and her hair was tousled all around her face. She had a I-just-got-lucky glimmer in her eye.

Riley hadn't fared much better, and she almost cringed when she saw the hickey on his neck.

"Sorry about that." She touched the mark that she'd left on him.

He glanced at it in the mirror and shrugged. "I like it when you forget the regs and lose control."

Tessa considered that for a moment. "Is that what happened here?"

"Among other things." He touched his mouth to hers. "Things we'll discuss when I get back."

Yes. When he got back. And Tessa refused to believe that he wouldn't return.

This mission had to be successful because the alternative was unthinkable.

Mercy, how had things come to this? She was a trained agent. Good at what she did. Twice she'd nearly been killed in the line of duty.

Yet this felt different.

Terrifying.

Something that was well beyond anything she'd ever experienced. The stakes were higher than they ever had been, and that sent a painful ache spiraling through her.

She caught the front of his shirt when he started to move away. "Here are the rules, McDade. No heroics. Definitely no diving in front of bullets. Do what you have to, but duck when the time comes."

Riley eased her hand from his shirt, kissed it and slipped on his shoulder holster. "I don't dive in front of bullets. Not purposely anyway."

"No, but they do have a way of finding you." Her voice lowered. Not by choice. But it was the only way she could force out the words. "Don't let that happen this time."

He looked as if he might argue with her. Or remind her that danger was part of the job. But he didn't. Riley took the *nice* way out and tried to soothe all the fears. All her doubts. "I'm tough as nails, Tessa. By tonight, this will all be over. I promise."

There was no way Riley could guarantee that, but Tessa clung to his promise anyway. She came up on her toes, to give him one last, farewell kiss, but the soft thudding sound stopped her.

Riley's gaze flew to hers, just a split-second glance.

And they both drew their weapons. Riley hurried to the right side of the window, the spot nearest the door. Tessa took the left.

She listened, trying to pinpoint the direction of the sound, but before she could do that, the phone rang. Not Riley's cell phone.

The phone next to the bed.

Riley shook his head, a signal for her not to answer it. Not that she had any intentions of doing that anyway. For one thing, it would give away their location.

And for another, it could be a trap.

The caller could be trying to lure one of them into a specific containment area so they could be shot. Of course, for that to happen, gunmen would have to be positioned outside the window.

Too bad that was a possibility.

"Do you see anything?" Tessa whispered.

He peered out the edge of the curtain. "No."

The phone continued to ring, the shrill sound echoing through the otherwise silent room. Finally it stopped and, out of the corner of her eye, Tessa saw the message light begin to flash. Someone was obviously trying to contact them. Probably not her father.

Well, maybe not.

He did have the name of the hotel and would have tried to call if something had gone wrong.

Or if he'd been trying to warn them.

Oh, God.

She didn't even want to speculate at all the things that could have gone wrong.

The ringing started again. Tessa tried to block it out, just in case it was a diversion meant to distract them.

She glanced out the window, as well. Sunrise was still at least an hour away, but the streetlights allowed her to see that the sidewalks were deserted. It meant nothing, of course, because Fletcher's men could easily be hiding.

When the phone stopped ringing a second time, the message light continued to flash. Her instincts told her that it was important. Critical, even. But she hated to risk Riley's and her lives on her instincts.

"Stay put," she whispered to Riley. Anticipating the worst and hoping for the best, she eased down to the floor and crawled toward the bed, out of direct fire if it were to come from the window.

Still staying low, she reached up, grabbed the phone and pressed the button to retrieve the message.

Or rather *the* message.

"Pick up when the phone rings again," the caller insisted. Tessa had no trouble recognizing that voice. It was Beatrice. Fletcher's armed *receptionist*. "It's important. Your life depends on it."

"Beatrice wants to talk to us," Tessa relayed to Riley.

He cursed, and she could see the debate he was having with himself. But the debate didn't last long because the phone rang again. Tessa pulled the phone and its cradle onto the floor and maneuvered herself away from the nightstand. Away from the bed, too. Fortunately the cord was long enough for her to move it to her original spot near the window.

Tessa picked up the phone, but she didn't say anything.

"Good morning," Beatrice greeted. "I'll make this

quick. There are gunmen posted on the roof just above you. We have infrared equipment so we can see your every move. In case you doubt that, I can give you a summary of your activity for the past fifteen minutes."

Tessa looked up and heard another soft thump. A footstep, and she could almost see Beatrice smiling. "That's not necessary." Tessa pressed the speaker function on the phone so Riley could hear, as well. "They're on the roof," she relayed to Riley. "With infrared."

He jerked his head up and his eyes narrowed.

"What do you want?" Tessa asked the woman.

"I want to talk to you and Agent McDade."

"Right. What you really want is to try to kill us like you did at my condo."

"We didn't try to kill you there. We simply tried to flush you out. It worked, too. Our orders were to follow you from your residence and to keep you under long-range surveillance so we could see who else was involved in this."

Oh, God. Her father. He'd walked into a trap and she'd helped to lead him there.

"How did you find me?" Tessa asked. "How did you learn who we were?"

"You wouldn't believe me if I told you."

"Try," Tessa insisted.

"The hot-dog vendor near your headquarters

building. After seeing your photo, he was able to give us your first name, and we took things from there."

Riley had been right. The leak hadn't come from an agent. Of course, at the moment that didn't give her much comfort.

"I'm surprised your boss didn't come with you," Riley snarled.

"He would have liked to do that, Agent McDade. But he couldn't. You see, he had to establish an alibi in case I failed. We wouldn't want the authorities to be able to link this directly to him."

"But he doesn't mind you taking the heat for him." Riley tossed the words right back at her.

"Taking the heat is exactly what he pays me to do, and he pays me well so that I'm never tempted to betray him. Or disobey his orders."

Riley shifted. Just slightly. And brought up his gun to aim at the ceiling.

"I wouldn't do that if I were you, Agent McDade," Beatrice warned. "Because while you're aiming your gun at us, we have several weapons already trained on Agent Abbot. Not Glocks, either. But weapons that would eliminate her before you could even pull the trigger. One wrong move from either of you and she'll be the one who pays first for the mistake."

Riley's gaze met hers and the indecision she thought

she would see wasn't there. In fact, there was no in-decision. "Don't move," he told her. "And I mean it."

That was in direct conflict with the fight-or-flight instincts that were screaming through her. But with gunmen on the roof, fighting would almost certainly be suicide. As would an attempted escape. No, they were trapped. And as much as Tessa hated to admit it, their only choice was to surrender. Temporarily surrender, that is. Then they could look for the op-portunity to escape.

"So, here's the deal," Beatrice continued a mo-ment later. "You'll both come with me to see the doctor. He's anxious to meet with you again, to dis-cuss things—specifically the information you might have learned from the hidden computer files he had at the clinic. If you cooperate, we won't assassinate Commander Abbot when he arrives. Oh, or perhaps I should say—*now* that he's arrived. He's parked at the side of the hotel and is stepping from his car."

"And we're to believe you'll let him walk if we surrender?" Tessa asked.

"No reason not to believe me. Commander Abbot can't trace any of this back to Fletcher. We've deter-mined your father is no direct threat to us. Well, not unless you make him a threat by bringing him into this. Is that what you want?"

Tessa didn't trust or believe her. No surprise there. But either way, this was going to come down to a fight. If there was some chance she could leave her father out of it, or at least give him a warning that he was about to be ambushed, then the chance was worth taking.

"Time's up," Beatrice said. "Don't attempt to shoot the man who's about to come through the window. If you do, all bets are off, and all of you, including Commander Abbot, will die."

Beatrice had barely spoken the last word when Tessa spotted the man on the rappel rope. He dropped lower and gave the glass a kick with the heel of his combat boot. Seconds later he burst through what was left of the glass and landed on his feet. Just inches from them.

"Move," the heavily armed man ordered, hitching his shoulder toward the roof. "Both of you. We're leaving now."

Chapter Fourteen

The RV came to a stop.

Finally.

By Riley's calculations, they'd been driving for nearly four hours. First, in the van with the blacked-out windows that had taken Tessa and him from the hotel to a rural area in northern Virginia. From there, they'd been temporarily blindfolded so they could be moved into the RV.

Tessa and he had been searched for weapons and communication devices.

Beatrice had taken his watch.

And Tessa's.

In addition, the woman had confiscated the backup gun in his slide holster.

Tessa and he had no way to contact headquarters, no weapons and no clue as to where Beatrice and her team of hired guns were taking them.

So far, this plan of cooperating sucked.

Riley made eye contact with Tessa. She was at the front of the RV, a beefy guard on each side of her. She had on her poker face, her agent's face. No display of emotion, but Riley knew she had to be scared. Not just for her own well-being and the baby's, but for her father's, as well.

There'd been no reasonable opportunity to escape. None. And, man, had he looked hard for such an opportunity. Four armed guards, including Beatrice, had been with them at all times. Plus, Beatrice had locked the doors of the RV. Manually. She'd slipped the key into her pocket and then moved into the passenger's section up front.

In other words, away from him.

Riley figured that even with her measures, he could pick the lock. Easily. But so far, that opportunity just hadn't come. And it wouldn't as long as those two menacing guards were near Tessa, because a wrong move from him would only further endanger her.

By now her father had probably assembled all available agents to track them down. At least, if Abbot were still alive he would have done that. There were no guarantees that he was. Despite Beatrice's reassurance that Abbot would be spared, Riley knew the odds were against it.

They were in the hands of killers.

Reassurances and promises didn't mean a thing.

Beatrice exited the RV from the front and, a moment later, unlocked the door at the back. She had yet another guard with her, making a total of five. Not good odds, but Riley knew somehow, some way, they'd have to escape. No choice about that.

The newcomer led him out of the RV, jamming his gun into Riley's back. Riley glanced over his shoulder to give the gun-jamming guard a nasty glare and to make sure Tessa was behind him.

She was.

And she was already surveying the surroundings, probably looking for an escape path.

Unlike the RV, there were possibilities here. For one thing, it was out in the country. The massive house toward which they were being led was surrounded by formal gardens and beyond that, pasture complete with what appeared to be Thoroughbred horses. If Beatrice tried to confine them in one of the rooms in the estate, Tessa and he could perhaps leave through a window and slip into the garden. Then beyond.

Until he had Tessa far away from here.

For now, it was step one. A vague plan that called for equally vague action. One small opening was all Riley needed to put his plan into action.

They followed a flagstone path toward the front of the antebellum-style house, and Riley briefly considered a drop and roll. One that involved a distraction and then ridding the guard on his right of the high-powered rifle and the 9 mm tucked into his shoulder harness.

But again, there was Tessa to consider. And the baby. With her yards behind him, he wouldn't be able to give her a signal. Or if he did, Tessa might not interpret that signal in time to get out of the path of what would almost certainly erupt into a gun battle.

No.

That was too huge of a risk.

So, Riley kept walking. Kept looking. And he kept praying he'd be able to get her out of this alive.

With each step he had to fight off the images of Colette's lifeless body. But the images kept changing. He saw Tessa in her place, and it felt as if someone had clamped a tight fist around his heart.

The front door opened as they went up the steps. No guard this time. It was Fletcher.

The doctor smiled at Tessa.

And that clamp around Riley's heart became even tighter. So tight that he was afraid he wouldn't be able to catch his breath. He fought the effects. Fought to keep a clear head and to keep his emotions in check. Because none of that would help Tessa now.

"Welcome," Fletcher said. But it was no greeting. The chill coming from it was of Arctic proportions. The man was obviously riled.

Fletcher stepped back into the shadows of the massive foyer and, one by one, they all entered. Beatrice kept Tessa back, near the doorway, while Riley's guards ushered him closer to their *host*.

But not too close.

Certainly not within reach.

Fletcher might be unrighteously riled, but he wouldn't want to risk Riley snapping his neck.

"I'm afraid Beatrice lied to you," Fletcher said, directing his comment to Tessa.

Riley saw her blink. Her only reaction. She probably thought Fletcher had just informed her of her father's murder. She stood stoic, and she stared Fletcher right in the eyes. "Am I supposed to be surprised about that?"

"No. I guess not. But you might be surprised as to what she lied about."

"You brought us here to play twenty questions?" Riley offered.

That earned him a scalpel-sharp glare from Fletcher. "I didn't want to discuss files with you. Maybe you already figured that out?" Fletcher didn't wait for either of them to answer. "Because it doesn't matter what you found. It doesn't even matter if you passed that information on to others. Without the computer files, you don't have proof. And the files, I'm afraid, are gone. Destroyed."

Riley had expected that, but it still wasn't a pleasant thing to hear. Or to accept. This mission had been all about finding and retrieving evidence. Without it, they wouldn't have much of a case. Of course, that was the least of his worries now.

Escape first.

Then he could regroup and come after Fletcher another time.

The difference would be that next time Tessa wouldn't be involved. He'd see to that.

Fletcher took several slow, calculated steps toward Tessa, yet still kept distance between them. At least ten feet. Riley wasn't much closer, which put him out of striking range, especially since he didn't have a weapon.

"If you're concerned about the lack of evidence, you could always confess," Tessa dryly suggested to the doctor.

Fletcher's mouth tightened, and then he must have realized that would amuse her, so he smiled again. "All right. I confess. Among others, I killed an SIU agent. Colleen…." He made a circling motion with his left hand as if trying to recall information. "No, Colette. I forget her last name. Something ethnic, I believe. By the way, she begged me not to kill her."

And with that verbal dagger, Fletcher glanced at Riley before turning back to Tessa. "Will you beg, too?"

Her chin came up a notch. "Not a chance. And I doubt Colette begged, either. That's wishful thinking on your part. Or maybe you're just delusional. I hear there are medications that'll take care of that."

Despite the sarcasm, there was no emotion in her voice, but Riley felt each word slice through him like a hot stiletto. If he didn't do something—fast— Fletcher would. The SOB would kill her. Riley would lose her and the baby the same way he'd lost Colette.

Riley lifted his left eyebrow a fraction. A slight gesture that he hoped Tessa would notice. But if she did, she didn't respond.

She couldn't.

Because at that exact second, Fletcher turned his gun on her.

TESSA HAD WAITED for some kind of signal from Riley and she prayed that the raised eyebrow meant she was supposed to react. If not, she would have reacted anyway because judging from the expression on Fletcher's incensed face, he was within a second of shooting her. It no longer mattered if they were outnumbered or that they were surrounded by gunmen. To delay would mean they'd die. If they fought back, there was a chance.

A slim one.

But it was still better than the alternative.

Tessa kept her attention focused on Fletcher's trigger finger and tried not to think of her baby. Or Riley. Or her father. She tried not to think of anything but surviving this. Because if she survived, so would her baby, and perhaps Riley, as well. Right now though, they had to make it past this first critical step.

Tessa sucked in a quick breath. Mentally counted to three. And as she saw Fletcher's right index finger tighten over the trigger, she plunged to the floor.

She didn't go alone.

On the way down, she hooked her arm around the guard to her right and gave him a quick punch in the back to knock the air of him. Using him as a human shield, she wrenched the gun from his hand.

She aimed it at Fletcher.

Riley moved, as well. With the attention of the guards still in her direction, he dove across the room, crashing his solid body into Beatrice. Like Tessa, he put the woman in a chokehold and came up ready to fire.

But so did the others.

"Decision time," Fletcher said calmly, turning in Riley's direction. Judging from his now calm tone, he could have been discussing the weather instead of what had turned into a showdown. "If you kill me, they'll just kill you."

"I've made peace with my maker," Riley responded without hesitation. "Something tells me you haven't."

"But your death isn't the big issue here, now is it? It's hers." He tipped his head at Tessa. "Judging from the infrared scans of the hotel, she's your lover. As was the other agent, I believe. A pity that I should be the one who takes both of them away from you."

Tessa knew that had to push at least a dozen buttons for Riley. Dangerous, volatile buttons. His eyes darkened. His jaw turned to iron. She saw the pulse jump in his throat. And she half expected him to launch himself at the man who'd murdered Colette.

But he didn't.

Riley got up from the floor, dragging Beatrice up with him and, without taking his gaze from Fletcher, began to make his way around the room toward her. Not angry, stalking steps, either. But the movements of a man trained for just this sort of thing.

Since Riley was watching Fletcher, Tessa tried to keep an eye on the others. With the exception of Beatrice and the guard she was holding, the other four had their weapons trained on either Riley or her.

Not an ideal scenario.

There were several ways this could play out. The most obvious was a gun battle. Not her first choice since Riley and she were seriously outnumbered and were in the open with minimal cover. So that meant they had to attempt an escape so they could be in a better position to return fire. And there was no doubt in her mind that before this was over, they would have to return fire.

She prayed they had ample opportunity to do that.

"Let's go," Riley said to her when he finally reached her. He rammed his hand inside Beatrice's jacket, retrieved some extra magazines of ammo and shoved them into his pocket.

Tessa followed his lead, stuffing the one magazine she found on the guard into the back waist of her jeans. Still holding on to the man, she began to ease back. Not toward the front entrance that was blocked by the majority of the guards, but through the adjoining living room where there was a door leading into the gardens.

Riley and she went one step at a time, while carefully watching Fletcher and the others.

She didn't dare hope that Fletcher would let them just leave. No way. He'd kill the guard and Beatrice before he let that happen. Riley must have thought so, as well, because as they reached a pair of marble columns in the living room, he shoved Beatrice forward. Away from him.

He was fast.

Very fast.

He latched onto her hostage, propelled Tessa behind him, and dragged all three of them out of the entryway.

Fletcher fired.

Just as the three of them made it behind one of the marble columns. It was meager at best, but at least it was cover. A good thing, too, because the other guards began to shoot, obviously following Fletcher's lead and disregarding the life of their comrades. The bullets slammed into the marble, clipping off chunks that became dangerous debris.

Fletcher ducked behind the foyer wall and Beatrice scurried behind a sofa. The other guards fanned out, each finding their spots in the foyer so they could continue to send their barrage of fire at Riley and her.

With a single shot, Riley took out one guard. Without missing a beat, he thrust their hostage into the open, dragged Tessa up from the floor and scrambled toward the side door.

Since Riley was returning fire, Tessa reached up, opened the door and bolted outside. She didn't run until Riley was out of the house, as well. And they began to sprint in the direction of the formal gardens.

They only made a few steps before bullets plowed into the ground around them.

Tessa spotted the two gunmen on the roof, but it was too late.

A bullet slammed into Riley.

Chapter Fifteen

Tessa didn't think. She couldn't. Even though she knew Riley was hurt. Instead she forced herself to react, to rely on her training so she could get them out of a dangerous situation.

She dropped to one knee. Took aim and eliminated one shooter on the roof. Then the other. That left only one guard, Fletcher and Beatrice.

She heard Riley curse and she risked a glance, praying that he was all right.

There was blood on his right arm. His shooting arm. God, he was bleeding.

Tessa latched onto him and got them moving. Fast. Behind a statue of some woodland goddess. Not the best cover, but it would have to do.

"How bad is it?" she asked Riley. She kept her attention fastened to the roof and the door so she could make sure Fletcher, Beatrice nor the remaining guard got the drop on them.

"I'll live."

That had better not be lip service or some come-back to reassure her. But in case it was, she looked at him again. Just a glimpse. And, yes, there was blood, but it didn't seem to be spreading too quickly.

Thank God.

Still, that didn't mean everything was okay. They had to get out of here. And Riley obviously needed medical attention.

"Don't you dare step out in front of any more bullets," he snarled.

"I could say the same to you. And don't bother to mention the baby. Because, believe me, I remember I'm pregnant. But I also know that I want all of us to make it out of here. That *all of us* includes you."

His silence meant he was considering that. "Then let's get the hell out of here."

Easier said than done. But Tessa preferred to be on the move since it was only a matter of time before the guard came running from the house to pick up where his slain comrades had left off.

Riley caught her arm and maneuvered her again so that she was on the *safer* side, behind the goddess and sheltered by a clump of shrubs. Tessa didn't bother to tell him that she should be at the point. After all, she wasn't injured. But arguing with Riley would not only be a losing battle, it was also a dangerous distraction.

They didn't need anything else going against them.

Together, they backed away from the goddess. Easing behind the shrubs, Tessa took a moment to check his wound again. She'd seen worse. Much worse. But because this was Riley, it caused a pain to settle in her chest. In that moment, she'd never hated anyone as much as she hated Fletcher.

"Stay with me," she heard Riley say.

And he wasn't just referring to their physical proximity. When Tessa briefly met his gaze, she saw that he'd noticed her examining his injury. He'd also probably noticed her renewed ire aimed at Fletcher.

"I'm with you," she promised.

Such a simple assurance, but she was more than a little surprised to realize that she meant that on every level possible. She was with Riley. Her heart. Her body. Probably her soul.

Mercy, the timing was all wrong for that revelation.

"Two choices," Riley said, calling her attention back to their more immediate problem. He reared up, for just a second, and fired a shot into the door where they'd exited. No doubt done to discourage anyone from leaving that way, as well. "We can run for the woods. Not my first preference because we'd be dodging bullets the whole way and there's no telling just how long or how hard that run would have to be."

"Our other choice?" she asked.

"We split up. I stay here to cover you and return

fire. You make your way around to the back of the house to the RV. Then, you get out of here."

She quickly thought that through. "Not without you, I won't."

"You can call for help."

When Tessa saw some movement behind the door, she fired a shot at it. "This isn't negotiable, Riley. I'll get to the RV, but I'll drive it back here and pick you up."

He mumbled some profanity. "God, you're stubborn."

"So I've been told."

He mumbled more profanity and shook his head. "Okay, third option. We both make our way to the RV and try to escape. Then, we'll call headquarters so they can get someone out here to lock down this place and take in Fletcher."

While she considered that, Tessa did another survey of the roof. She also checked the doors and windows of the estate that looked out onto the gardens where Riley and she were hiding. Together, they would make a much more obvious target. They'd be easier to track. And they'd be easier to kill if Fletcher had that infrared aimed at them.

"I know what you're thinking," Riley whispered. "So here's option four. I go first. You lag back and cover me. And eventually we both make it to the RV."

It was a logical plan.

So why did she want to resist?

Tessa didn't have to explore that for long. She knew. The answer was Riley.

"I'll be careful," he said, as if reading her mind. "You'll be careful. We'll both do what we've been trained to do and we'll all get out of this alive."

She nodded, partly because she wanted to believe what he was saying and partly because she knew they couldn't delay any longer. Every additional second was a second that Fletcher would be using to regroup.

Riley got up from the ground. Still crouching, he tipped his head toward the back of the estate. "We'll go that way. Use the shrubs for cover and then make our way around to the front as fast as we can."

Tessa nodded. She knew there would be no turning back. No time to second guess this plan or any of the others they'd already discarded.

No time to tell Riley that she was in love with him.

But she was.

Tessa suddenly knew that with absolute certainty.

He cursed and, for a split second, she thought he'd seen the emotion on her face.

"Get down," he shouted.

Tessa saw then what had caused his reaction. And it wasn't her expression. The last guard and Beatrice had moved to the roof. Tessa heard the zing of a bullet as it collided with her own weapon, the impact sending the Glock flying from her hands.

She dove to the side, behind a concrete birdbath, to avoid a second shot that would have almost certainly hit her squarely in the chest. Riley scrambled ahead of her, behind a bench, and came up to return fire.

But so did the gunmen.

The bullets began to bombard them. Everywhere. All around them. Tearing at the shrubs and gashing into the birdbath and the bench. The sound was deafening. A barrage of noise, chaos and danger.

And she was unarmed.

Worse, the direction of the shots changed. Suddenly, Beatrice and the guard seemed to be shooting only at Riley. From what she could tell, none were coming her way.

None.

By the time she realized the impact of that, of what it likely meant, it was too late.

Tessa saw the movement from the corner of her eye. Turning, slowly, she saw the gun. And the man holding it.

Dr. Barton Fletcher.

THERE WERE too many shots.

Riley hoped that didn't mean Fletcher had managed even more reinforcements. Not good. Because he wanted nothing to delay his plan for getting Tessa out of here.

Seeing that gun fly from her hands had taken ten

years off his life. Thank God she'd gotten out of the way of that second shot. Now maybe she'd stay down until he could try to contain the situation.

"Are you okay?" he shouted to Tessa.

His shout brought on another hail of gunfire. He cursed when one of the bullets caused a jagged piece of concrete to slash across his left cheek. But Riley barely noticed the sting from the minor injury. He barely noticed because he realized Tessa hadn't answered.

"Tessa?"

Nothing.

Absolutely nothing.

He shifted, grimacing at the stinging pain in his arm. He tried to sort through the thick foliage to find her. And he hoped that the reason for her silence was simply that she hadn't heard him. Yes. That had to be it.

Because she couldn't be hurt.

Unfortunately she wasn't by the birdbath.

Riley maneuvered inches away from the bench, and still didn't see her.

The shots stopped.

Just like that.

Without warning.

And the silence settled in around him.

He didn't dare call out her name again because it would give away his location. That was perhaps the very thing Fletcher was waiting for him to do.

Talk about feeling helpless. Tessa was out there. Somewhere.

Maybe too hurt to respond.

Riley forced that thought aside and concentrated on what he had to do. But it was like being in that surveillance van all over again. No matter how much he tried not to, he was reliving Colette's death. He'd let her down... But he wouldn't do that to Tessa and his child.

He came up on his knee, positioning himself to lunge across the narrow clearing so he could get to the area of the gardens where he'd last seen her.

She had to be there.

She just had to be.

"Looking for someone?" he heard Fletcher ask.

Riley snapped to the sound of that voice, his weapon ready to fire. A weapon he soon realized he wouldn't be able to use.

Fletcher stepped out from behind a section of thick shrubs. And he wasn't alone.

He had Tessa.

God, he had her. His arm was curved in a chokehold around her neck, the barrel of his gun pressed directly against her right temple. One shot would almost certainly be fatal.

"The estate once belonged to a Colombian drug lord," Fletcher commented. "He was a very cautious individual. Fortunately, there are escape tunnels and security cameras all over the place."

And that explained how Fletcher had managed to sneak up on her. Tessa wouldn't have been able to hear him, not with the noise from the gunfire.

So the shots had merely been a diversion.

It made sense. Well, it made sense to a killer. Fletcher wanted to do away with them himself.

Without the risks to him, of course.

That's why Beatrice and the guard had been on the roof. If Tessa or he made one wrong move, Fletcher would kill them. And if he failed, then his gunmen would do it for him.

"Here's the deal," Fletcher continued, inching even closer. "If you come out now, Agent McDade, and surrender your weapon like a good boy, I'll allow you and your lover to say goodbye. If you refuse to cooperate, I'll simply kill her where she stands."

And he would, Riley didn't doubt that.

So he stood, and in the same motion, tossed his gun onto the ground in front of him. Surrendering, but it was close enough that he could make a dive for it if he got the chance. And one way or another, he would get the chance.

"Make your goodbyes quick," Fletcher insisted. Gone was the calm demeanor. The doctor now seemed overly eager to pull that trigger.

Riley looked at her. Confirming first that she hadn't been injured and then checking her eyes to see what she had in mind. Because, heaven help them, they needed something.

"I love you," she said.

Riley stared at her and mentally replayed what she'd just said to make sure he hadn't misunderstood. He apparently hadn't. Because Tessa repeated the words.

Oh, man.

Fletcher laughed. "This is *so* perfect. Instead of the Baby Maker, maybe my patients should call me the Match Maker."

The man was still laughing when Tessa mouthed, *Now.*

It was the cue Riley had been waiting for. He didn't waste even a second. He dove for his weapon just as Tessa rammed her elbow into Fletcher's stomach.

Fletcher staggered back. Just slightly, but didn't let go of his gun. Tessa dropped to the ground, kicking the back of Fletcher's legs so that he fell.

One of the gunmen on the roof fired. Not at Fletcher or Tessa. But at Riley. Riley did some firing of his own. Instinctively he fired two shots. A double tap of the trigger and took out Beatrice and the last of the guards.

Riley pivoted. Just in time to see Fletcher shove Tessa, and then try to aim his gun at her. Riley fired. Not to kill. Not this time. His shot smashed through Fletcher's hand and the man howled in pain.

Still, Fletcher reached out again, ready to grab the gun.

"Part of me *really* wants you to do that," Riley informed him through clenched teeth.

Fletcher stopped and stared at him.

"Because I'm having a serious fight with my conscience right now." Riley inched closer. "The only thing I want more than justice is you dead. So I'd think twice before giving me an excuse—any excuse—to kill you."

Fletcher angled his body and looked at him. And for a moment, Riley thought he would go for it.

Riley thought he might *go for it,* as well.

But then he saw Tessa.

And Riley knew there were some things more important than getting even. More important than living in the past. More important than anything.

He kicked Fletcher's gun away, so the man wouldn't be able to reach it and, choking back the emotion that he knew would be in his voice, Riley read Dr. Barton Fletcher his Miranda rights and placed him under arrest.

Chapter Sixteen

Taking in a deep breath, Riley shifted the ficus plant to his bandaged arm and pressed the doorbell to Tessa's condo. He waited, more than a little alarmed that he was starting to sweat.

Both literally and figuratively.

He had no excuse for the literal part—a cold front had moved through the area and it was only a few degrees above freezing. The D.C. wind was whipping at his calf-length black leather coat, and his ears were going numb. The figuratively part, however, well… that was a whole different story.

During the past forty-eight hours since they'd collared Fletcher, a lot had happened. First, they'd learned Tessa's father was alive and unharmed. And the Evidence Response Team had discovered that Fletcher's estate was well-equipped with surveillance cameras. Dozens of them. The SIU could thank the previous owner, the Colombian drug lord, for that. The entire shoot-out, including Fletcher's confession that he'd murdered Colette, had been captured on tape. From multiple angles. However, it would only take one of those *angles* to insure a murder conviction.

Also within the past forty-eight hours, Riley had already had a dozen discussions with Tessa.

Too bad all those discussions had been in his head.

Or in the mirror in his bathroom.

Now that the debriefings were over and their mandatory forty-eight hours apart had come to an end, it was time for the real thing. A real talk. And therein was the problem. Even after all those practice sessions, Riley still didn't have a clue what he should say to her.

The door opened. And she was there in front of him. Wearing a bulky strawberry-colored bathrobe, she had a thick white towel draped around her hair. She'd obviously just stepped from the shower, and she smelled like some kind of exotic flower. That scent, coupled with the sight of her, sent his testosterone levels soaring.

Oh, man.

He wondered if he'd always have that reaction to her. That punch of lust, all swirled together with every positive emotion he'd ever felt.

Talk about potent.

He'd experienced a lot of powerful things in his life, but Tessa Abbot was at the top of the list.

"How's your arm?" she asked, eyeing that particular area of his body.

"Better." Thankfully the bullet that'd sliced across his right forearm hadn't caused any real damage. "I'm already ninety percent healed."

One of her eyebrows lifted. "I heard sixty."

He shrugged. She'd obviously been talking to her father. "It'll be ninety by the end of the week."

"My guess is seventy."

"Let's split the difference and go for eighty." Riley forced himself to quit gawking at her and handed her the ficus plant. "It's a housewarming gift. Well, sort of. Your father told me they'd finished the repairs to your French doors and bedroom, and I thought that was worthy of a remodeling gift."

Tessa made a sound of pure delight and smiled. Dimples flashed. And that gave Riley another serious slam of testosterone.

As if he needed more.

"You bought me a live plant." She said "a live plant" as if it were a priceless gift. He made a mental note to give her things more often.

"Try not to this kill one, okay?" Because her teeth were starting to chatter from the cold, he stepped inside and shut the door. "I hear regular watering and sunlight help, but that could be just a nasty rumor."

She smiled again and set the ficus on the floor. When she stood up, however, she slid her hand inside his coat and ran her fingers over his butt. "Still there, huh? I guess the chief didn't chew too much of it off."

"Nope. In fact, he gave me a promotion of sorts. I'll be head of covert and deep-ops training for rookies."

"So it's true. You can take out the 'of sorts.' It's a definite promotion. One where your penchant for breaking rules won't cause you to get regular butt chewings from the chief."

Since she let her touch linger on that particular part of his anatomy, and since she slid her fingers to his stomach, and lingered there, as well, it took Riley a moment to get his eyes uncrossed. "Spoken like a smart-ass in training. A little more time with me, Tessa, and you'll qualify for full-fledged bad-girl status."

Her smile faded. "I don't think I'm the bad-girl type. No tattoo, for one thing. And then there's my, uh, situation."

"Badass isn't all about tattoos," he quickly informed her. "It's in the eyes, and I'd say you've got that glare thing down pat. Definitely a mission commander's glare."

He'd hoped that would make her smile return. It didn't. "You make me sound so…attractive."

"You are, and that wasn't meant to be sarcastic." He shook his head. "Still, it sounds inadequate. But you are. Besides, who says a pregnant woman can't be both smart-ass and hot? I think you're hot, and you'll continue to be incredibly hot throughout this pregnancy. And afterward."

Tessa didn't have quite the reaction he thought she might have to that compliment. She closed her eyes for a few seconds, sighed and sank down onto the bar stool.

"I ran a home pregnancy test this morning. Just to be sure," she said. She unwound the towel from her head and tossed it onto the bar. Her damp blond hair fell onto her shoulders.

And she didn't say anything else.

Her silence, coupled with the sigh, caused Riley to start sweating again.

"Well?" he prompted.

She moistened her lips. "The test was positive."

Riley released the breath that he didn't even realize he'd been holding. Okay. That got his mind back on track, and he knew their discussion couldn't wait.

"You seem, uh, relieved." But Tessa didn't give him a chance to respond to that. "Look, Riley, I've been giving this a lot of thought. Heck, I've been practicing what to say to you, and the bottom line is—"

"You practiced?"

She blinked, nodded and dismissed it with a wave of her hand. "Trust me, it didn't help," she mumbled under her breath.

He knew exactly what she meant.

"It's just...I don't want you to feel obligated," she continued. "A baby is my version of the white picket fence and a perfect life, but there's no way I want to drag you into this." She stared at him. Frowned. "Now, you look upset."

"Well, hell, maybe because I am. First of all, you didn't drag me into anything." He stalled a bit on the second part, since he knew what was at stake here.

Simply put, Tessa didn't need him.

She was independent. Smart. And had just been made a mission commander in SIU. It was a desk job, but one that would give her a nice cushy income. Unfortunately, Riley wanted her to need him. Not for a paycheck. Heck, not even for sex or moral support.

Okay, maybe for that.

But he wanted Tessa to need him as much as he needed her.

And that was a lot.

"Something happened back at Fletcher's estate…" he started to say, hoping it made sense. Because it sure didn't make sense zipping through his head. "Things got clearer."

Her face relaxed a bit. "Because I'm sure inserting my foot in my mouth wouldn't be very appetizing, I think I'll just ask you to explain."

Riley debated which way to go with this and decided the direct approach with minimal words was the best. "I'm in love with you."

Every muscle in her face froze and those blue eyes seemed to double in size. "You love me?"

That was it.

Just those softly repeated words and more of that stomach-tightening silence.

"I love you," Riley confirmed. "And it's the real thing, Tessa. I'm sure of it." Mercy, where had the air gone? "I seem to remember you mentioning something at Fletcher's estate about loving me. Of course, I realize that could have been the heat of the moment, because you thought we were going to die." He shook his head again. "And I'm really babbling here. Say something, please."

She didn't say anything, but she launched herself at him. Fortunately, Riley was right there to catch her because she jumped into his arms. Well, his good arm anyway. "I was afraid this was just sex to you."

She took the words right out of his mouth. "Not even close."

And that earned him a kiss. A long, hot, clingy kiss where she wound her arms around him and didn't let go.

It was better than any white-picket-fence fantasy. It was paradise.

"Until I heard the results of that pregnancy test," he managed to say, not easily, "I hadn't known just how much I wanted a child. Or how much I could love. Now, I know."

When she pulled back, there were tears in her eyes.

"Oh, man. I made you cry." Riley immediately started to wipe the tears away.

"It's happy crying. It means you did good. You said just the right thing."

The tightness in his chest eased up a bit. "Then say it right back to me."

"I love you." She kissed him on his cheek. "I want you." She kissed him again. On his mouth. "I need you."

And she really kissed him.

"Even better." Riley fought for his breath and decided he didn't need it anyway. "There are only two things I want. You and this baby. Okay, maybe four things." Heck, he might as well go for broke. He slid his hand inside her robe and discovered she was very much naked. "I also want to make love to you all afternoon. Maybe even in bed." He eyed the sofa. Which was a lot closer. "Or not. That's negotiable."

Tessa, who was obviously a mind reader, was already leading him in the direction of the sofa. She was also nibbling on his neck and peeling off his jacket. "And the fourth thing?"

"Marry me."

Her quest to get him naked stopped. Because he had his hands all over her, he felt her muscles stiffen. "Marry you?" she repeated.

He nodded. "I'm not really comfortable making that a question. Because I don't want you to say no."

She smiled. And it was dazzling even with the happy tears. "Then this is your lucky day, McDade. Because you can have all four things. Me, the baby, some great sofa sex, and yes, I'll marry you."

She sealed that promise with a kiss. And Riley sealed it right along with her.

It was indeed his lucky day, and Riley would do everything in his power to make sure that luck continued for a lifetime.

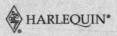

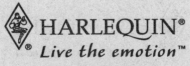

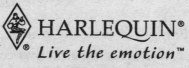

If you enjoyed what you just read,
then we've got an offer you can't resist!

Take 2 bestselling
love stories FREE!
Plus get a FREE surprise gift!

Clip this page and mail it to Harlequin Reader Service®

IN U.S.A.
3010 Walden Ave.
P.O. Box 1867
Buffalo, N.Y. 14240-1867

IN CANADA
P.O. Box 609
Fort Erie, Ontario
L2A 5X3

YES! Please send me 2 free Harlequin Intrigue® novels and my free surprise gift. After receiving them, if I don't wish to receive anymore, I can return the shipping statement marked cancel. If I don't cancel, I will receive 4 brand-new novels each month, before they're available in stores! In the U.S.A., bill me at the bargain price of $4.24 plus 25¢ shipping and handling per book and applicable sales tax, if any*. In Canada, bill me at the bargain price of $4.99 plus 25¢ shipping and handling per book and applicable taxes**. That's the complete price and a savings of at least 10% off the cover prices—what a great deal! I understand that accepting the 2 free books and gift places me under no obligation ever to buy any books. I can always return a shipment and cancel at any time. Even if I never buy another book from Harlequin, the 2 free books and gift are mine to keep forever.

181 HDN DZ7N
381 HDN DZ7P

Name _____ (PLEASE PRINT)

Address _____ Apt.#

City _____ State/Prov. _____ Zip/Postal Code

Not valid to current Harlequin Intrigue® subscribers.

Want to try two free books from another series?
Call 1-800-873-8635 or visit www.morefreebooks.com.

* Terms and prices subject to change without notice. Sales tax applicable in N.Y.
** Canadian residents will be charged applicable provincial taxes and GST.
   All orders subject to approval. Offer limited to one per household.
   ® are registered trademarks owned and used by the trademark owner and or its licensee.

INT04R   ©2004 Harlequin Enterprises Limited

Like a phantom in the night comes an exciting promotion from

HARLEQUIN®

INTRIGUE®

ECLIPSE

GOTHIC ROMANCE

Look for a provocative gothic-themed thriller each month by your favorite Intrigue authors! Once you surrender to the classic blend of chilling suspense and electrifying romance in these gripping page-turners, there will be no turning back....

Available wherever Harlequin books are sold.

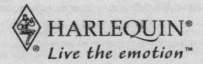

HARLEQUIN®
Live the emotion™

www.eHarlequin.com   HIE3